SWIMMERS
IN WINTER

SWIMMERS IN WINTER

FAYE GUENTHER

Invisible Publishing
Halifax & Prince Edward County

Library and Archives Canada Cataloguing in Publication

Title: Swimmers in winter / stories by Faye Guenther.
Names: Guenther, Faye, 1980- author.
Identifiers: Canadiana (print) 20200203894 | Canadiana (ebook) 20200203908 | ISBN 9781988784502 (softcover) | ISBN 9781988784533 (HTML)
Classification: LCC PS8613.U4472 S95 2020 | DDC C813/.6—dc23

Edited by Bryan Ibeas
Cover and interior design by Megan Fildes
With thanks to type designer Rod McDonald

Invisible Publishing is committed to protecting our natural environment. As part of our efforts, the cover and interior of this book are printed on acid-free 100% post-consumer recycled fibres.

Printed and bound in Canada

Invisible Publishing | Halifax & Prince Edward County
www.invisiblepublishing.com

We acknowledge for their financial support of our publishing program the Canada Council for the Arts, the Ontario Arts Council, and the Government of Canada.

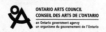

SWIMMERS IN WINTER

I CAN'T READ LUCILLE'S SMILE. I know her name, and that's all.

We only met a moment ago, in a back room so dark you have to look twice to tell anything. She stepped out of the shadows into the copper light pooling around the bar and ordered another drink. Her face and hair streaked gritty with illumination. She leaned there and waited, inside the music, breathing in the perfume and smoke and the deeper scents of the strangers all around, watching for who was looking.

Moving toward her meant being willing to fall first.

Around us, the room is a small ocean of girls, rough, beautiful. It's long after midnight, and Lucille and I stand side by side, a sliver of space between us. We watch the dance floor, drinking hard, while girls hook and pushers work the sidelines. Women's voices slap and swing their laughter up against music from the record player looked after by Elegant Ivan, the bartender, who knows most of the patrons by first name. In the centre, they're dancing so close.

I drink deep and gesture to Lucille with my hands. Words spill away from me and I scramble to catch them, raising my voice, to hold her attention through the clamor, the catcalls, the sweet murmurs.

I tell her I'm Florence and that I do a little bit of everything. They call me a downtowner, because deep in the city is where I'm at home, living in a ramshackle building with a hole in the roof that lets in the birds.

"That sounds familiar," Lucille answers, laughing low and calm, a little resigned. Brushing her dark hair away from her round face, she sways a little on her feet, as if the music has caught her at the waist. She glances past me at the endless action. The top button of her blouse has come off, leaving behind a few loose black threads and a soft window of bare skin below her neck that grows wider as she moves.

"First time here?" I ask her.

"Hardly. Yours?"

"These girls are my crowd," I proclaim, hearing the harsh brightness in my voice. How it must sound to her—flaunting and eager.

Lucille turns to me, searching my face. "So you make music? What do you play?"

"A little bit of everything. Mandolin, piano, harmonica."

Hearing this, she starts telling me about a kind of travelling show she plans to do the next year, a musical tour, describing it as if there's a stage in her mind. Lucille talks like someone who never runs out of what there is to lose.

"Nowadays, I play alone," I reply with a smile.

And now the stage in her mind disappears, and she sees me instead. Me and the restless crowd of strangers.

Lucille leans back as if to let us all go. She takes out a cigarette and I light it for her. "Maybe you can write me a song," she says, her voice dipping with the weight of what she wants.

I nod, as if it might keep her from drifting away. She reminds me of a girl I used to know. Magda. Her slow burn and fast flame.

Lucille touches my hand, the one holding the lighter. She rocks slow onto the balls of her feet, her lips a soft *oh* in the smoke. "I plan to take my band from here to New York," she says. "We'll go everywhere and back again."

Then she steps closer, filling the space.

"Want to come with us, Florence?"

She remembers my name, so I kiss her, like it's something to say. And after that, I get ready to kiss her again, slow and long, the burnt sugar taste of her mouth soaked with rum still on my tongue.

But just as I feel her breath on my face, my thoughts turn to escape.

We hear them before we see them coming.

A swarm of cops—at least thirty—move in fast, the flush of their pale skin, charged by force, hats pulled low, thick uniforms, truncheons lifted.

Dancers, still in each other's arms, stumble as they turn toward the sound. The music continues as if stuck in a dream, behind barks of "Police! Move back! Get up against the wall!"

I reach for her hand and push hard, through the panic of the room, toward the fire exit.

In the shock of frozen air filled with sirens, women hastily pull on coats, then spill from the heavy door into the alleyway behind Dundas and Elizabeth. Lost and intent, like swimmers in winter, they dive into the cover of darkness through heavy drifts of fallen snow.

I turn to ask Lucille which way is home, but she's already gone. I stumble around in a circle, searching for her, calling out her name once, twice, toward the escaping forms.

Possessions lie scattered on the icy ground, dropped or forgotten in the rush to get away. A single glove. A pair of glasses with cracked lenses. An orphaned scarf. An undone string of pearls. Cigarettes and cigars, still long. Beer sloshed on the snow. Flasks bleeding gin or brandy.

A woman screams in the street, a tremor that tears up

and down, burning. It could be Lucille's voice. I almost move toward it, but stop myself.

At the other end of the alley, paddy wagons and an ambulance rush north to Dundas, red lights flickering on the snow before disappearing. The cops could find me any second. I could be arrested, beaten in the snow. Hidden behind the building, away from public view, the cops will swing their boots, fists, and sticks harder against the skin and muscle they find, even breaking bones. I've felt their blows before, pain that bends the body into itself, my head crushed against my heart.

All I can do is run.

Survival is instinct to me, an old demon-friend. I let her enter, let her come.

The late-night streets in Chinatown are unusually deserted, hollowed out by the glow of streetlights, and the shop and restaurant signs alight with letters. The farther I get from the Continental Hotel, the quieter and more still the city becomes. Just the muffled crunch of my soles hitting the snow, almost in rhythm with my heart.

A stray dog noses and burrows at ripped bags of garbage tossed against the back of an old building. He's a blue-grey hound, I see through my watering eyes. Hungry and hunting. I stop to catch my breath. It blooms thick as smoke in the cold. The smell of cooking wafts by on steam rising from an exhaust pipe. We lift our faces to the warm, oily scent, the dog and I, and when he sees me, another searcher, we watch each other for just a moment.

"Hello, beautiful," I whisper.

He barks in warning and takes off down a narrow passage between two buildings.

◊

Can't remember a time when I wasn't covered in the traces of leave-taking. The thinnest skein of flight was always wrapped around my limbs.

I come from a family of five children. As the eldest, I was expected to help look after them all. Which I did. But I was restless.

That's what they called me. *Restless*.

All five of us played instruments. I was the first one my father taught to read music. My mother would sing. We played music to entertain the neighbours: dance tunes, folk music, little classical numbers father collected the scores for that had to be mailed to us from far away.

I learned that when I played a song, sadness and troubles would halt—for a while.

◊

I came to Toronto the summer of '42, when there were still good-paying jobs for women at the John Inglis factory on Strachan Avenue. Manual production, making weapon parts and other equipment for the war effort, while the young men were gone to fight overseas.

I was a musician, but I needed the work to pay my own way.

Once alone, the body has a way of arguing itself into places it needs to be. I started looking for other girls like me, and as it turned out, there were plenty of us doing factory work.

The factory was where I'd met Magda, but it was in the bar room at the Rideau, on the east side of town, on Jarvis

Street—where I really got to know her, standing alone at her own pleasure.

Our first summer, we would hide out under a thicket of trees in Allan Gardens, a couple of blocks from where we had first found each other. We couldn't believe no one stopped us as we walked arm and arm along the streets, our hands dipping around each other's hips, two girls surrounded by a city's rising thrum, its young muscling of new concrete, glass, and light. Though we felt ourselves naked to the world, we always made it into the park without seizure, without arrest.

The first time Magda leaned toward me and undid her clothes in the shadows under the spread of branches, it untied a knot inside me. The intersections of her body were a revelation of shifting curves. The space almost became ours, its underbelly of leaves. My Magda. I remember her open palms and the way she filled me. I remember her mineral taste in the dark.

At the start, every new lover is a story you choose to believe. A story about where you have been, where you're going. A pack of cards shuffled, reshuffled, dealt again.

◇

In this world, protection is a necessity. The more I look like myself on my way to the bar, the greater the chance I'll get stopped by the cops—for "loitering" is what they say, for "acting and looking like a man," when all I'm doing is walking freely in a public space at night. The charge of causing a disturbance now allows them to arrest and detain anyone after dark. This new Chief James P. Mackey and his dirty Inspector Herbert Thurston want all of us women gone. It has been in the newspaper, and I know it firsthand.

Just my presence is enough of a trigger for the cops, enough to get them shoving me between them, taunting me with threats, calling me by names I shudder to hear, names that make me the target of violence.

I'm not afraid of a fight. What I fear is how badly I could be hurt, because I'm all that I have in this world. My father and mother are gone, and my sister and brothers out of reach. I can only rely on my own body and mind, and the ability to use them. Nothing else. So I must look after myself, whatever the cost.

One night, the cops left me curled tight on the ground, coughing up blood. I felt a rip in my chest, and I knew that their kicks and punches had broken something inside, something that might be too deep to heal.

But though I told myself that time would be the last time, I do not dress or present myself as someone other than who I am.

I will not change out of fear.

Instead, I carry a knife. And I've learned escape routes. How fast I've got to run.

◊

I head back to the boarding house, near Kensington, where I'm renting a small room. Time to pick up the pace again, race against my fear. I stumble on patches of ice, catch myself. Under my wool coat, I feel my skin dampen with sweat, my heartbeat quicken, my lungs tighten from the cold. Each escape, I encounter this familiar exertion laced with terror.

There's no knowing when the bar raids will happen. You always have to be ready. I do my drinking, my smoking, in expectation. Even in the company of the most beautiful woman in the room, I'm ready to run.

It's the undercover lady officers who are the most trouble. I lay down my defenses with them. Four times, I've been a breath and a touch away from arrest. Each time, either following a kiss I was willing to lose myself in, or after I've tried to talk to them all evening at the bar, or when they've danced up against me slow for five songs straight, they suddenly pull out a badge as if it's a weapon.

I like women who know the worth of their weight, women who build themselves solid like planets. But these informers are dirty and lawful magicians. Either they're the best of all actors, or I swear I've tasted and smelled real lust, felt it in how their bodies moved with mine. I wish I could cut open my mind so they can look inside, see the bright rooms and dark spaces. It isn't sick in there, or twisted. I know it's not what they expect to find.

I should have reminded myself of that tonight, right from the start: any sweetheart, with her tenderness and her mercies, could be an informant, working for the law or otherwise. To survive, you've got to keep out of the affairs of others, even when you're in their beds. Guard yourself. Take everything in stride. The less you reveal, the less there is to lose.

I don't know if Lucille was arrested tonight. I can't go to the police station to try and find out. I don't know her last name, or if she would have told it to me if I'd taken her home. After all, I wouldn't have told her mine. Not yet.

Now I don't know if I'll ever have a chance.

◇

Weeks go by. Spring arrives, sliding in, wanting and breathless.

Just as I summon the courage to return to the back room of the Continental Hotel, they shut it down. After four raids, all its girls are finally driven out. They'll find another place.

But much like the way I repeat certain melodies by heart, I find myself returning again and again to the intersection of Dundas and Elizabeth. Something pulls me back to the fitful movement here, strangers leaving their traces in my tune as they walk away. In the evening, I play my songs on each of the three corners opposite to where the shell of the Continental Hotel stands. I serenade its boarded-up back room, windows like blinded eyes. It's smaller than I remember.

As I busk here through the rush hours, workers head home, cabs and trolleys run by, memories fly back. These city walls of scabbed brick are my backdrop; my music quiets as their grainy surfaces soften in the dusk.

Everywhere, industries that employed us during the war have been shuttered. But the factories didn't stay empty for long. Fancy new appliances and the goods of peacetime are assembled on the production lines now, and most of the jobs have been taken back by men. I take what I can get. It's clear to me how much is changing.

I can almost hear the restless rhythm turning in time with my fingers against the strings of the mandolin. Melodies trembling to an end. Other ones beginning.

As I play, I try to become the sound, the way a drop of blood enters water. Glancing away from the cycle of passing legs, I search the faces, drawing out my tune, for a chance to catch sight of Magda. The way I remember her.

Or is it Lucille, still new to me, in the looseness of a run-down coat? Just another stranger, except that she remembered my name.

All this time they make us spend on disappearing—but here we are.

FIGHT OR FLIGHT

AWAKE IN THIS SLUMBERING HOUSE. My night light's out, but it's moon time. She moves so slow in the sky, even I could match her pace. Through the window, she floats in the deepest, darkest blue. I try to fix her in my sight, but my weak eyes let her go.

What am I doing standing here? It will take me a while to remember.

Turn back to the room that holds you.

What is it now? Middle of the night? Could be. Night of middles, round and thin. Night of doorways, standing here holding on to this solid frame, to keep mine from falling.

Right here, right now, at the doorway to hell.

Only joking.

It's where they told me I'd go when I was young. Did I listen? Not at all. Nothing stuck. I forgot their threat. Buried it in the background.

"We'll stick it to you," they said. The words landed somewhere, but not where I listened. Instead, I waited for someone to hold my face in their hands, to tell me: "Remember what our music is, Magda."

Now, I try to find this music and drink it in like water.

They say all you need in this life is breath and love. Or is it bread and roses?

And when your time here is up, there's barely a rehearsal, so small a pause, a breath, right at the entrance to the stage, to reckon with your spirit before you walk on and let it rip.

This is how it is, the oldest woman in me imagines: you walk on, see the faces, a few of them familiar. You see the bright lights and that's it. You're gone. No first note, no sound. As you open your mouth, your spirit leaves. There it goes, rising higher, over the audience, above their hands—if by chance they raise them up to try and touch it. Try to hold on.

Quiet friend who has come so far,

I imagine, but I can't say if it will be that way for me at the end. When I slip away, will it be sudden and swift? Will there be someone to hold me in their arms as I go?

feel how your breathing makes more space around you.

They say that you might have to climb to get to heaven, but to get to hell, you just walk right in. I'll tell you what: no one's going to see me climbing any steps to heaven, that's for certain. Not with these hips and knees. They're like the rusted gears of a bicycle left out in the rain. Sticking, clicking, hurting.

No, I'll just go straight in, and keep going down the block.

You never know what a corner will turn around for you. Sometimes, it's a stranger who waits for your company, collar up, cap low, cigarette still aglow, feet so tired and used to running for escape when the need arises. They won't meet you until you notice them first. They'll wait and see. Take their time.

I was always one to notice, because—because that's what I was like.

Did a friend tell me so? More than once?

In the kindest way, sure.

"Do you mean I was generous with my attentions?" I finally asked her. "That I was giving?"

"Well, you are that too."

Tell me what I am tonight.

Sometimes the corner you round, on the street or in your mind, will turn you a terror, and you're so sick in your speed you may not notice the terror is catching up.

No.

Let this darkness be a bell tower
and you the bell.

No. I'll turn away if I can manage it. Take this slow slide-step forward and away. See? It's the looking back that makes me lost again.

Oh, these aching hips, these knees that every day seem to argue back harder.

This body is an oyster and my life is a shell. I fear I will be pulled out in the end, unwilling. Torn from my casing. I will feel every bit of the letting go. Tearing. I will be alive to the swallowing, and the pain of the end will ruin me.

Or will I be slurped into the last of all mouths, gently, tenderly? A tasty morsel, a bit of flesh. A reminder of real desire as I go. The ocean, my original bed.

For now, I'll be the old woman who uses the door frame as her walking stick. Leaning on it while the bell tolls. While I toll it. Age hasn't stolen much of my hearing, though it's managed to nibble away at the full range of my voice. With a blessing, they say, comes a curse. I've always known that.

There's a trick to it, I used to believe.

Find the blessing that's worth it. Then run like hell from the curse.

I know this sound. It shudders the air around me. Ringing, ringing. Louder than before. But let me be the bell. Quiet friend, let me be the bell.

Let this darkness be a bell tower
and you the bell. As you ring,

what batters you becomes your strength.
Move back and forth into the change.

Who wrote that?

Which poet was the first who found those words as beautiful as love inside his mind?

Of course, I forget. Only I know they are not mine. That peace and its great beauty are not yet mine to speak.

They say the entrance to the stage is always open if you know how to find it. This is my last stage, but I'm not ready for an encore. No, not prepared to be left alone out here, solo until the end, left out in the downpour, waiting for time to wash itself over me, only to find I'm all dried out.

What have all my acts amounted to?

Small and forgotten, most of them, and so early on, too late to go back and rearrange enough of my choices to erase the mistakes. If I had the chance to do so? Honestly, about half—well—at least a third of my past would vanish.

Here's the thing: I have always chosen to put down my defenses when faced with the kind of attention I wanted. Yes, you could call that a fault, but it's also required for the stage; it's one part of the work of seduction. I learned this when I was a singer and a tambourine player. The crowd waits for you to notice them, and only then do you start to give them what they want, reveal yourself to their attention. The choices of rhythm and speed for this revelation are mostly yours, until they're not—but it's the transaction of desire the crowd is really looking for, and what they want to believe is the end result, the payoff, every night.

They want what they think is your heart, but only if you make them believe they can know what it contains.

This became instinctive to me over time—an instinct grown out of habit more than intention, though I will admit it was first born of passion. But no one could own me. That was what I promised myself every night, on and off the stage. I was my own keeper, my own maker, and it would always be that way.

Life has its own current, though. No matter your will, there's the rush and the undertow. The truth is that I'm not a swimmer. If I learned how to stay afloat, it was only because I knew what drowning felt like.

Let me remind you I'm still very much alive tonight, in the liquid of the moonshine, bathing in what is made rich by the sinking of one lucky penny. Up to my neck in a little reflecting pool of night wishes only. The depths turn to shallows, and the shallows turn to shadows. Will I come ashore, washed up?

Where am I?

A little room of my own where at least I can close the door. I can't afford to live on my own now, so I've moved in with my great-nephew. A rug on the floor, books on the shelves, a radio I can sing along to. My window looks out on a street that rattles with traffic once or twice during the day and folds in on itself at night when I draw the curtains closed—it's not my type of street, too still, but it passes the day to watch it. Surrounding me in this semi-detached brick house is his young family.

My great-nephew teaches at a university, never knowing if his job—like the one I had at the munitions factory during the war—will be there from fall to winter to spring. He got me a book of poetry from the university, reads it to me now that my eyes are almost all out of vision. He thinks the fine-tuned words will give me comfort, thinks I still feel enough to need it.

Which is true, if feeling is the mind's last song. I do sing it. The brain's a precious thing. Floating in its juices in the skull, not so unlike the oyster in the shell.

I'm surprised and grateful that he engages my mind, by which I mean he understands I still have my own will. I think he's curious what I might do next.

What was the poet, and who was the book? It travels to me across time and space, the sound of the poet's words takes me turning round and round, until my feet leave the ground. I float. I close my eyes—there's no need to look. I go. No, not up any stairs to heaven. Instead, the words take me to the stranger on the corner and the touch of their hand. The words are the witnesses to my confessions.

Move back and forth into the change.
What is it like, such intensity of pain?
If the drink is bitter, turn yourself to wine.

In this uncontainable night,
be the mystery at the crossroads of your senses,
the meaning discovered there.

I think I know well what it is to turn myself to wine, to not let myself drown, or at least to drown differently. But who else am I in the mystery and in the meaning?

Don't make me go out on the stage yet. Let me hover here for now. I'm not ready, and finally I'm old enough, almost eighty years, to know it.

Well, listen—

I won't go out there unless I can bring the band with me, for one last sheltering storm of sound. The dancers are waiting, just beyond the circle of light where I stand, with their eyes on me. Florence is there, her fingers to the mandolin strings. I haven't thought of her in ages. She and the other musicians, they watch me for a sign. My inhalation, enough for the first note to pitch and lift its song, my right foot raised, they wait for my toe to touch the floor, the tambourine to come down. The first beat of my final encore.

My untidy bed unmade yet again. Look what's in it. All the undoing, every wave in my original bed, coming to break against the shore.

Move back and forth into the change.
What is it like, such intensity of pain?

I steady myself in front of the closet's full-length mirror and try to fix my eyes on the old woman I see in reflection. She wavers for a minute under my gaze.

I've made it this far, out of the doorway and into the closet. Ha!

On a hanger inside is a men's suit.

I reach up heavily, my arms and shoulders moving under water, and manage to get it off the hanger, to hold it up and recall how it felt when I had it on.

In the mirror, I blink back, growing indecipherable.

The suit is longer than me, long to the floor, the ankle cuffs drag more than they used to. I'm an old woman whose world has grown several inches taller. Now, great-nephew can lean over and kiss the top of my head as he says goodnight.

"Good night, Magda. We can read again tomorrow."

"Good night, my son." Oh, but that was a slip of the heart, or the mind, or the tongue.

He doesn't seem bothered, but then, I can't quite make out his face in the lamplight.

"Sleep well, Auntie."

"I wish you every dream."

Was that only earlier this evening? Or else I'm plummeting backwards. Gravity sees there's a job for me to do down below. As if this body hasn't done enough labour, in war and in love. I'm sunk by gravity, the pressing mask of night seeks to flatten me. It takes me lower to the ground. How will I breathe when I get there?

But see how it is. I can still notice the world around me, yes, the faces in the crowd. I'm open to distraction, and this is what leads me to pause. To notice. To meet their eyes.

I can't deny that it has led to the wreckage I built. And the shelters I've found.

Down there, spread against the earth, I'd begin to admire the edges of the blades of grass as if they were the young scaffolding of an emerald-green cathedral. Life. One of the great hues of the planet. One I've never seen this close before. Not these blades of grass in particular, and not any cathedral—well, in pictures, but not in person, because the church threw me from its holy halls as soon as it saw my fatal flaw.

The error at the heart of me. That exquisite error that changed my life. Its invitation, which was, simply, to live.

What is it like, such intensity of pain?
If the drink is bitter, turn yourself to wine.

In this uncontainable night,
be the mystery at the crossroads of your senses,
the meaning discovered there.

What time is it? Who will keep it?

The musicians raise their hands to the instruments. Florence is there and she waits with pleasure, with mine in her hands.

She is that perpetual first real lover.

But stop.

Maybe I'll seek another face I can recognize, in the crowd gathered here to watch.

Quiet friend who has come so far,

No, there's no one else tonight.

So, who will find me in this dimming mirror?

Squinting as though this will help me to see, I slide my wrinkled hand with its curvature of blue veins along the collar and the sleeves of the suit, first the left one, then the right. I touch each button and the dark leather belt of the pants. The buckle, grown dull, still carries its own weight—no rust yet that I can see. I pull the zipper up and then down. My hands shake despite me. I move them across the fabric to feel how threadbare and worn it is in places, but still complete.

Did the suit belong to me? I had more than a few sets of men's outfits, both suits and factory clothes.

If I'm honest, I was always taking them off to climb into someone's arms.

When I look back to my reflection in the mirror, I can almost see a lover standing beside me, the glow of the lamp glinting in their eyes.

I blink and we drift out of focus. I blink again and I can't see them there at all.

Who do I have left to hear my confessions?

When I was young, what I longed for most was to be able to make my own choices, to be someone of my own making. Keeper of myself.

The Second World War came, I was twenty-one, and like many girls tied up in uptight Hogtown, biding their time, I began to work. While the war raged, no man would marry me, which meant I had no reason to start a family. Factory work, the war effort: that was the new path a girl could clear through her wilderness when she left home.

I wonder, though, if I would still be alone had I had babies to mother. Would they be here now to keep me company, keep me tethered longer to my life? Would they be my anchor?

A selfish wish perhaps, an unanswerable question—the kind I'm good at asking. I'd raise a glass to it, every time.

If not for Florence, how would I have known myself? I learned from her, before she let me go. A lover teaches you to understand the limits of yourself, and how to lose them. Both the limits and the lover. I could drink to that truth too.

But enough of drowning in spirits.

Florence was the first girl who tried to call me home. We met at the factory, where we fell into step and pull and lift with each other as machinists on the assembly line. I can picture her now, in her last-ditch tight coat and worn-down boots. Bold and honey-eyed.

We tossed ourselves away in relief at the end of each day, long after dark, when the streets cleared out. Usually, we headed to the basement of the Silver Lounge, crowded with girls, or to the Rideau, which is where she first kissed me, leaning up against the wall in that smoke-and-laughter-filled room, for what seemed like several glorious hours. Later, in the warmer months, we'd leave the bars for the park. Allan Gardens was a big sprawling patch of green, and we went there for cover, though it was never safe enough to stay for long.

Rolling in the leaves at night. Her mouth above mine. Her hair brushing my face like a filament of stars. I let her break me down, and I buried my fears beneath her, filling her with new hunger, almost too quickly, because we had no cover. We both acted like thieves, the way we took from each other, thinking we had found a home.

Florence was the girl who opened me up to the night. I loved the music she made on street corners, turning tunes to passersby, or sitting on the old bed in her small rented room, playing songs for me to sing with a voice that did not know its limits.

What can I hear? It's like a melody in the night air. There it is again. The sound of a mandolin. Florence's music. Or is this a dream to me too?

I'm used to the night. Sleep hasn't come easily for a long time. Was I dreaming, just a minute ago, of standing there in front of the mirror at the closet door? Or, did I find my way back to bed, only to wake again? I can't recall.

I lie here on my back in the dark while shapes and shadows float past my eyes, as if I'm a diver looking up at the surface. There's a little pale light coming from the window, and I can't tell if it's from a streetlight or the moon.

Listen, the music is louder than before. Her melody strains.

In this uncontainable night,
be the mystery at the crossroads of your senses,
the meaning discovered there.

I tried on a men's suit and jacket for the first time when I was twenty-four.

We'd started a band. I was the one singer so far and we needed to find another, an alto, for harmonies. Florence thought a lot of me, but she knew my voice had its limitations, so she sought another voice to complement mine, to really make it sing.

The suits would be our stage look, she said, and we could wear them offstage too. I put one on, and it just felt right. The suit of my desires. I walked the length of Florence's rented room in it. She told me the clothes were castoffs, but didn't tell me how they'd come to her. Wearing it, I moved with a feeling of buoyancy and endurance—what they now call confidence—as if I could swim a long distance, as if I could dare to make it from one far shore to another.

Florence sat on her cot in the corner, watching me. I can still picture her distinctly, leaning back, relaxed and intent, her hand poised with its cigarette over an ashtray that rested on a pile of musical scores. She wrote that music, as I recall. It was her freedom in the floating world.

"I'll get more suits," Florence said abruptly, as was her way. But I knew well enough by then that she would've given me the clothes off her back.

"This is the only one you have?" I asked.

"Go on then, take it. Just be careful when you wear it. Especially out on the street."

I could not refuse her gift.

Let this darkness be a bell tower
and you the bell. As you ring,

what batters you becomes your strength.

I'll ask for a truth now, because I'm alone.

Why couldn't Florence have stayed with me a little longer?

The war gave us no centre to hold onto; it spun us out. We were still young, everything had happened so fast, and we were working, making our own money. How were we supposed to settle with so little time to do so?

On top of that, we were made to feel wrong for who we were. It often felt like our own flaws were all we had to live for.

But listen to me now: I was my own keeper. I was trying to be my own maker.

It was like crossing a bridge over the flow of life—that river that threatens to rise in its terrors and wonders.

Toward the end of the war, our world crumbled. The jobs disappeared, the police cracked down on us; our music rose and then faded. The men who had fought were slowly returning, or not returning, lives gone and other lives broken. Their victory a small flag in the midst of the destruction and desecration that war brings.

Three of my brothers had left to fight, and only one came home. His son was born two years later, and that son had a son, my great-nephew. The only one in my family I've grown close to. Maybe the only one who cares.

Life can move so suddenly. The river rises, floods the bridge.

What remains is all I'm left with now.

But I haven't lived this long to be wrecked by what has already been done.

And if the world has ceased to hear you,
say to the silent earth: I flow.
To the rushing water, speak: I am.

It was at the Silver Lounge that Florence introduced me to Hannah, another singer. Hannah had a range deeper than mine, richer and more open, an alto for sure. No interest in a tambourine, though—I'd have to play that one alone.

Hannah told us she was new in town and looking for a place to work. She'd sung with a travelling band for a while. When they passed through Hogtown she decided to stay, to see whether she could make a life for herself underground in this dirty, conservative town. She'd lost her own little brother in the fighting overseas and was carrying that grief on her back. Struggled with how heavy it was to bear.

What I remember most is the flicker of recognition in her solitary eyes. She looked at Florence closely that first night, but not in a searching way, not seeking to know what was in her heart. It was more like she was open to waiting.

I liked the lines that carved her out. Weary lines, but full of decision, as though she'd chosen to come so far just to be herself.

Something in me understood why Florence might've longed to go with her.

Florence was doing all the talking, sharp and swift. "So we'll have a practice next weekend, at eight back here before the bar opens." She then went silent for a minute, probably thinking about how to arrange it.

Hannah looked over to me, then back to Florence.

There was something about Hannah that night that was utterly new to me. I could tell she was distracted, but the attention she rested on each of us felt both gentle and full, and also like something I couldn't hold.

Thinking back now, I'd say it felt like she was witnessing us, and wasn't asking for much more than that.

I noticed too that Florence's eyes kept failing to not meet Hannah's. I knew what it was to fall into someone's eyes, to weave an alibi full of holes to cover up desire. So I shot Florence a look that said, *I'm watching*.

But then Florence touched my shoulder once, twice. A tender gesture that caught me by surprise, as we were rarely light of touch with each other. She said my name before she wheeled away. Was she calling to me, asking that I follow?

I wished Hannah good night with a stage smile and turned to go.

"You're always looking," I said to Florence when I caught up to her. "Looking for whatever you want."

Well, maybe that was true. When we met, I was the only one who caught her eye. But I must've known, even then, she had a glance that didn't rest for long and yet so often seemed like it was ready to be found.

I wanted her to convince me I could count on her, but she didn't. The words escaped her.

But you are mine. That's what I wanted to hear. We had been fighting plenty, almost to the brink, and I'd begun wondering if she would leave me.

It just made me fiercer.

"I bet on nothing," I leaned in, my voice low and hard with what I knew to be my own hurt. "But I took a chance with you."

"Don't you know the difference between lust and something deeper?"

"No words," I told her. "There are no words for this. What you're doing."

She was getting ready to walk out on me, then and there. I knew it. But I also hoped that she expected me to follow.

Was that love?

I wanted to think I was still the chance she would take. I waited for her to speak but she didn't seem to have an answer.

I recalled the crowd we'd played for that night. All the strangers' faces. I thought of Florence on stage with me, her profile. I'd tried to hold our melodies well and stay focused, though in one of the songs, I'd begun a wrong verse, the last one, and I had to hastily skip back to the middle of the song. Florence shook her head when it happened, but kept the rise of the chords steady into the chorus. There was some whistling from the audience and laughter. Usually, I appreciated a lively response from the crowd, the way they pulled and hollered at the songs with happiness and abandon, but tonight it troubled me.

Had Florence really been in love with me?

Now, looking back, she seems so young.

We were still standing there, staring at each other, when the front doors burst open and the bar raid began. How many nights had an intrusion like this happened? Too many to count.

In the space of a breath, Florence spun around and headed for the back exit, her mandolin in its case held aloft like a treasure in her arms. She went without waiting for me, never even seemed to hesitate.

Shocked, I didn't think to run right away. Not until an officer grabbed me from behind. Desperately, I bit down hard through the skin of the hand on my shoulder, and when it released its grip, I threw myself toward the back of the club and darted away out the backdoor.

I was turned inside out with terror. But there's power in fear, if you channel it through action. I couldn't feel my feet hitting the pavement. The sirens sliced the air to pieces as we scattered away.

More than anything, I was worried the police were chasing me, that they were catching up and closing in. I'd been chased before. I ran until my legs hurt worse than the fear in my chest.

I could still feel where the officer had gripped my shoulder hard enough to bruise. I gulped in the fresh air, and silently spoke a desperate wish to not be seen—pretending at invisibility, the way you do when you feel hunted, even if you're already down the street and around the corner. Begging at fate to make what scares you disappear.

The summer we met, after the first time we'd escaped a police raid, Florence had said, "They can't steal us from ourselves. We're both still alive. We're together. So breathe. Come back to yourself." That was the moment I began to fall for her. But she hadn't said it especially for me. That was just how Florence lived.

As I slowed down, I became more aware of my surroundings, those familiar streets of escape. I didn't want to go home, so instead I went to Allan Gardens, to the place Florence had taken me after that first raid, and those many other nights that followed. Lone figures stood here and there in the park. Some leaned against the tree trunks as if expecting an eventual train, in no hurry, lost in their own thoughts and feelings. Their faces were mostly hidden to me behind branches and leaves, but I knew they watched me pass, then turned the other way, their stolen glances either consoling or indifferent.

I told myself I was not afraid. I was used to being the outsider, the shadow eater, the night walker.

As I stepped along the path, I remembered how Florence and I had sat on the grass side by side, the June moon low and all over us in its solitary poses. I remembered wondering what she saw, what she thought of me that first night: the limits of my life so far, all that I hadn't yet seen and done and known. Would she somehow come to understand me as the police did, see me painted over with the same names that they had for me, as something ugly or sick, as less than human?

There are strange, panicked tricks our minds play when we're faced with the question of love. We search out any alibi. We tie ourselves in knots.

I thought then that if I was going to say something to her, I had to share some shameful truth about me. I had to confess to her the truth of what others thought of me.

Perhaps it was also that I had a taste for the dramatic, and I wanted her to listen to it.

But Florence shook her head. She didn't want to hear my past regrets and my fears in that moment.

So instead I asked her, "What can I give you?"

She looked up past the branches to the sky, the moon splashing its light everywhere, the dampness of the night air filling her mouth, her throat, her lungs, as she breathed it in slow.

"What doesn't hurt so much," she said.

Then she turned and looked me all over. I tried to meet her eyes. I don't know what she saw there, but she smiled unconcerned, with a trace of reassurance. "Whatever you'd like," she added.

She turned away again to her own thoughts. A private grin on her lips. There was always a bit of a trickster about Florence, a lust for survival.

That first night, I'd wished time could slow as I brought her pleasure instead of pain, that she would be no thief with me, that what I gave her wasn't stolen. I'd wanted her to let me take her in. I'd looked for hope in Florence's eyes, a balm for the feeling of my own shame. I'd searched for a way to soothe my mind.

A stirring in the trees nearby startled me from my memories. I needed to keep moving.

There was no moon to be seen in the sky above, just a dusting of old stars beyond the city's young, encumbering blaze of electric light.

I imagined Florence beside me. I thought of how she'd played at the bar: louder, harder, more jubilant in her sound than the rest of the band combined. She played as if she could sense another raid was coming, and that they would try to shut the place down for good.

I tried to believe that if I looked for Florence, I could find her again.

Has love been the breathing I have taken for this life? Like most of us, I've done so, deeply. But only a few times. In this, we do not have a choice.

Quiet friend who has come so far,
feel how your breathing makes more space around you.

In the noise of their world, where do I go?

Sometimes great-nephew's children come in to visit. I try to sing for them, old Auntie Magda singing her ghostly tunes. The littlest one gets up to dance to the melody on feet she just learned to walk with, moving back and forth like she can feel the rhythm that was there with us on stage all those years ago. They laugh, the children in my room. I do love to hear their laughter.

Their mother, I remembered her name earlier. She visits here, this tiny island of a room, to take the children back so I can rest, scoops the littlest one up. Short haired, soft framed, and I confuse her with my own mother for a minute.

My mother told me once that I was born waving my fists, a fighter.

"Like almost every child," I replied, stubborn.

"No, you were born a mad one. That was you."

Mama, they were fists of joy.

If she were here now, I would go to her.

Tell me again where I am in this night of middles, this life I see drifting by. The earliest time curves back to me. The older memories are so strong. The first melody Florence ever taught me. I can still feel what it was like to sing its song.

"I'll sing again for you soon," I tell the children.

Their mother waves.

Goodbye, sweet ones.

I look outside my door as it closes.

That's life happening there, Magda. Life unfolding around you. The loudest kind of life. Their noise never stops. It rushes by. But at least you can still hear it happening.

At least for now, they seem to hear you.

And if the world has ceased to hear you,
say to the silent earth: I flow.
To the rushing water, speak: I am.

Lately, my surroundings have begun to fall away, their definitions softening. This is something I can't refuse, no matter how I try. I find less and less to hold onto. My strong prescription glasses don't change the fact that I'm losing my vision. It is dispersing—the way dreams go, travelling out of reach, out of orbit.

Tell me where I am tonight.

Sitting up in this unmade bed. Hips aching, I gently swing my legs to the floor, then gradually lift myself to my feet. Each step is slow and deliberate as I move toward the door.

What am I doing here?

There's a draft in this space. It shivers me—though isn't it spring yet? My favourite time of year. Shouldn't the night be mild?

And what about my thoughts?

If it's true what great-nephew says, that I have seen a lot, why should I be surprised at the visions coming now? Why should I refuse the encore if the crowd wants me back? If Florence is waiting, ready to play, fingers suspended?

Halfway down the hall, the floor moves like a footbridge, shaking with my frail-boned weight to throw me over. Each of us takes ourselves down in the end.

But I still have a wall to help keep balance as I shuffle, sliding each foot along it. These hips and knees—no touch can soothe now.

After a few more steps, I'm standing again in front of the full-length closet at the end of the hallway. I'm pulling at the closet door—it only needs a gentle tug to open. Was I just here before? Just a few minutes ago? It's hard to recall.

Shall I go back? To a new beginning?

In the stillness of the night, the creaking of my footsteps on the wooden floorboards announces my returning existence. Is it walking if you move as slow as the moon floating in the sky?

I rub my eyes, leaning against the wall to hold myself upright, swaying unsteadily for a minute, expecting brightness. Of what? An afternoon sun? But it's only the dimness of the hallway that I find instead, and down the hall my bedroom with its window.

Turn back to the room that holds you.

Let me open up the window here to find a little last air before I wake. Where's the latch? The window holds the moon, or is it a streetlight? Or the sun rising? I'm not sure which.

I can see the pale light wavering on the floor in rhythm with another idle dream. For a minute it fades, and then comes back into focus. I blow it a silent kiss, all that is left for me to give.

What else will know me here, besides the light? Is it song?

Look what I've forgotten.

I'll get my old suit of desires from the closet. Lift it from the hanger to put it on. A humble suit but it served me well. I'm ready for the stage now, to sing again for you. Please, quiet friend, hum a little music as I go, to bring me into tune. As I stand here bent and breathing. Just breathing.

Quiet friend who has come so far,
feel how your breathing makes more space around you.
Let this darkness be a bell tower
and you the bell. As you ring,

what batters you becomes your strength.
Move back and forth into the change.
What is it like, such intensity of pain?
If the drink is bitter, turn yourself to wine.

In this uncontainable night,
be the mystery at the crossroads of your senses,
the meaning discovered there.

And if the world has ceased to hear you,
say to the silent earth: I flow.
To the rushing water, speak: I am.

      "Sonnets to Orpheus, Part Two, XXIX"
      Rainer Maria Rilke
      translated by Anita Barrows and Joanna Macy

THINGS TO REMEMBER

EVA

I HAD A JOB IN THAT DINER BEFORE CLAUDIA DID. It only seems like she brought everything with her. But I was there first, alone. Day after day in that steaming kitchen, we worked as dishwashers and short-order cooks. We were on our feet for hours, wearing obligatory hairnets and knee-length aprons tied over tank tops and old jeans stained to a fade. Our bare feet squealed across the linoleum floor in fluorescent sneakers from BiWay or Thrifty's. After a year, those shoes became lace-up combat boots we wore even in summertime. Claudia's apron usually lay flat against her after she tied it on like armour.

See how much I remember?

All I wanted from the future was that it would be different from what I'd already known. I only saw the tasks at hand as things tying me to the present—tethered there, impatient.

When I knew Claudia better, I told her, "This is what you do on the way to something else. The trick is to always keep moving. If you look back, be ready for anything." When no one else was watching, we covered our ears with our hands, elbows angled outward as if to ward off double-fisted blows, keeping our eyes wide open.

It was a way to both escape the past, and face it down.

But from the beginning, Claudia had tunnel vision. Her

hands were like tools when she worked, adept and precise. Sure, she might have made mistakes, but it was all practice. That's all it was for her.

Whenever the other dishwasher went on his endless breaks, I'd watch Claudia move away to stand over the big metal sink basins. She would brace her hips against them and pummel gooey traces and grease streaks of food off the dishes and down the drain. Her fingers gripped the hose, with its steady jet of hot water, like she was holding onto a rope to pull herself up.

I wanted the focus she had. I wanted to know how it felt to have her attention.

◊

We shared almost every shift.

"How are you?" I'd ask, not looking, waiting. A question so ordinary it's easy not to give a real answer. But you need to start somewhere.

"Doing fine," she'd say. "Yourself?" Handing me silence above the constant clang and rush of the kitchen.

For a long time, I knew next to nothing about her. Our conversations were always cut off by a new task, a new order, the entrance of one of the other cooks or a server.

◊

One morning in mid-October, a few of the staff called in sick. Another cook just didn't show. "I'm ready to quit," he'd told us the previous week. "I've got something better lined up."

Fewer of us there meant more work, but also more space, and Claudia took the lead. The manager didn't notice until mid-morning. He walked into the kitchen and looked around as if he'd lost something, then paused to find us doing prep for the afternoon.

"You can see I'm short-staffed today," he said, "so you'll have to handle the lunch rush."

Maybe you didn't notice we just got through breakfast, I thought to myself.

"No problem," Claudia said.

"Keep the customers' orders coming steady," he warned her. "No gaps."

After the lunch prep was done, those of us working in the kitchen decided we would start taking our breaks as the orders began coming in, instead of waiting until it got real busy.

The others took their turns first, leaving just Claudia and me. I said to her, "You're so quiet today."

It was only half true. Claudia always seemed quiet.

She looked up at me as she made grilled cheese sandwiches, buttering six slices of bread on both sides, moving in a flash, two fingers red from a recent burn.

"I'm concentrating," she said.

I smiled. "You're not bored?"

"I don't get bored." Claudia put down the knife and reached for the pan.

"Really?"

"No. There's always something to do."

"You mean in this job?"

"In this job. In life." She turned back to the sandwiches.

"Huh." I thought about it for a minute. "It's funny to hear someone say that. I think a lot of people would get bored."

Her focus was back on her hands now. She laid the sandwiches out with intention, side by side, neat in the pans.

"You know what it's like when you've got all these things to figure out, like everything is piling up and you can't get to it?"

I thought I understood. I tried to, as I stirred the big pot of cream of tomato on the back burner. "So what's on your mind?" I asked her.

"Memories, I guess. Nothing bad. It's just that they never go. There's a pile of them there, but they're all out of reach."

She frowned as if in apology, but her eyes were bright. I wanted them to dare me.

"Like songs that get stuck in your head?" I tried.

"No, not really like that." She laughed warily. "Because you can sing a song to yourself, and it'll eventually disappear. Get replaced by another one, I guess."

Another order came in. Tuna salad. I went to the fridge to get out the bowl we'd prepared that morning, and extra mayo. She hovered the spatula over the pan of grilled cheese, a rare moment of stillness. I went and stood beside her, watched the butter and orange cheddar sizzle with heat.

This was basically against the rules. We were always to be doing something. Not standing still. Not waiting.

She began to flip each sandwich, one at a time, briskly, with perfect aim. "These memories," she continued, "there's no story I can turn them into and retell. They're just flashes. Like, quick flashes. And then they're gone. Still in my mind somewhere, but I'm always getting further away from them."

"Try thinking forward," I said to her. "The past can wait because it's done. Think about the future instead. No one else is going to do that for you. Don't ask for permission either."

Don't ask for permission was a phrase I'd found in a magazine at the grocery store, or maybe someone had said it on television. I tried to make the words sound like they belonged to me.

The sandwiches were ready, so Claudia headed for the deep fryer. Almost every order came with fries.

I thought maybe she hadn't heard me, so I tried again. "Sometimes you have to take chances to get ahead."

◊

Later, I would offer her my own confessions—all of them in the past tense. As though my memories were shells that contained oceans. I told her things then that I haven't shared since. It was a relief, to turn myself inside out for her, heart in my mouth, then trail off.

I did that with Claudia. I told her the things I wanted to hear.

◊

That was how it began. Some worry or wish, which led to another, until they flew around my head like birds. It got harder and harder to hold them in, hold them down. I would rub my eyes to get rid of what fluttered there.

One day she asked me, over the wet rattle of dishes, what was wrong.

And I knew what it was. Not something wrong exactly, but something new.

I looked at her.

Claudia was taller than me by half a foot. She lifted her dripping hand from the sink to my curly hair and gently pulled. "You've got a bird's nest up here," she said, laughing, as a flicker of water mixed with soap suds landed on my face.

◊

I didn't know much about cooking when I first applied to work there.

The manager looked me up and down. "Ever work in a kitchen before, Eva?" he said.

I lied about working in three others before this one.

He kept squinting at me, so I crossed my arms over my chest and focused on a poster just to the left of his face, an image of the CN Tower puncturing the sky, with the words *See you at the top!* in punchy gold letters. But his eyes continued roving until something fell in the kitchen and he turned toward it, cursing.

Broken free of his attention, I reached for the strap of my shoulder bag and readjusted its weight. It held a two-litre carton of milk I'd found on sale, cigarettes, and some day-old buns and pastries from a shop on the corner. I was all out-of-pocket then, and betting a place like this would have leftovers at the end of the day, leftovers they needed something to do with. That's what made me walk in when I noticed the *Help Wanted* sign in the window.

"Okay, sweetheart," he said. Then his eyes were on me again, so I met them, and he looked away. "We'll give you a try. Be back here tomorrow, seven a.m."

He never did say *hired*, but I knew that I was.

Not long after that, I realized I was the only girl working in the kitchen.

◊

A month after I started, I saw the hiring sign was back in the window. Maybe business was picking up and they needed extra help?

I found that possibility hard to believe.

The kitchen was empty by the end of my shift. The morning and lunch rushes were over, and most of the other staff had gone on their breaks, leaving me to clean up before I could slip a few things in my bag and head home. I was leaning for a minute on the counter—to rest my arms, sore from the dishwashing and from carrying the piles of plates—when I heard the jangling of the bells on the front door. Then a voice, solid but cautious, in a girl's deep pitch.

I knew the manager was still standing by the cash register at the front of the restaurant, counting change. I wanted to listen, so I moved to stand just inside the entrance to the kitchen. I was worried about being replaced. I guess I was also trying to look out for her. Just in case. I didn't want him to try anything with someone who wouldn't know to be careful.

He told her he already had one pretty girl, and asked what he would do with two.

I caught a glimpse of her reflection in one of the mirrors along the walls that made the room seem momentarily endless. She cocked a smile: sudden, sure, and a little hungry.

I recognized it before I knew her.

Maybe that smile was what the manager thought he was looking for. Or maybe he realized, from the resumé she handed over, that she actually had enough experience and could find her way around a kitchen.

One thing I know for sure is that he underestimated her from the beginning.

"Eva will show you around," he said. Then he paused and called out to me. "Eva! There's a new girl starting today."

And suddenly she was walking toward the kitchen. Tall, with sloped shoulders, her hands in her pockets. I moved away so it wouldn't seem like I'd been listening at the doorway the whole time.

She barely looked at me when we said our hellos. Instead, she surveyed the space as if she could see some possibility that wasn't visible to me. I wondered what she thought of the state of the kitchen. Its chaos that I was supposed to wipe clean.

Even then, I was already craving suspense, when it was Claudia I was waiting for.

I watched as she forced herself to accept a hairnet from the cardboard box. Then I handed her an apron—a spare one I'd yanked from a hook in the broom closet, one smelling of ketchup and the laundromat—and told her that it would be deducted from her first week's pay.

That was when she finally looked right at me, down from her height, with those brown eyes of hers. The kind of eyes that go on and tell you something and then almost immediately look the other way in case you happen to hear what they have to say.

"That's messed up," she said quietly, shaking her head, "to have to pay out of our own pockets." She frowned.

I thought maybe she was trying to figure out how she could afford it. "Tell him," I said.

She didn't. But I noticed that she would treat that apron as if she'd earned it, as if it was made for her, even though any of us working there could've worn it.

.

Later, we stood across from each other at the counter, rinsing, peeling, and chopping carrots and potatoes. Their moist surfaces glistened in the fluorescent lights.

"Like a sauna in here, right?" I said to her. Claudia wiped the wet edge of her forehead and jerked a thumb toward the end of the kitchen facing out on a crumbling parking lot behind Yonge Street.

"Hotter in here than outside. Even with that back door propped open," she replied, as if it was a secret she was tired of keeping.

I wondered how long would she last.

◇

There were so many rules around us, spoken and unspoken, and we were both used to being told we had broken them. It was something we shared from the beginning.

But still, it grated on Claudia. Getting told she'd done things wrong. I think it was because she paid attention and noticed the hypocrisies, always deciding between whether to point them out or to prove herself despite them.

The thing is, except for when she was cooking, everything Claudia decided to do took time. A lot of time. No matter how fast life was moving around her, she moved slower.

I warned her that there are only so many opportunities, and they tend to change and disappear if you don't make a choice and run with it.

The two of us took the most blame under the manager's watch. He liked strong words and he would use them to get a rise out of anyone. More than once, he told us he should let us go.

One Sunday morning, when we were hungover and chopping potatoes for the deep fryer, he came in and saw that my hair was down around my shoulders. I tried to sweep it up in a bun when I heard him coming, but it was too late.

"Listen. You listen to me, now," he hollered. "There's no way I'm gonna let this kitchen get shut down by some goddam inspector because of you. You better clean yourselves up if you want to keep this job. I've said it before. I don't want to have to say it again, right?"

Our eyes took in the floor and then the ceiling, flinching at the clang of pots and pans, and at the bright fluorescents. I felt a sense of tired relief when he left.

I told myself that he wouldn't have the guts to fire me then and there because he still needed me, at least for that shift. I also told myself I didn't really care either way.

Claudia, however, looked disappointed—maybe in me, maybe in herself.

I wanted to ask her: *Why would you expect anything else from him?*

◊

A week later, I decided I wasn't going to seal my head in a hairnet anymore. The job didn't matter to me. I would not give it my loyalty. Instead, I wore a baseball cap into work, my hair pulled back tight inside it.

It was early morning. I found Claudia already there, alone, the first one to arrive in the kitchen. To my surprise, she seemed almost betrayed when she saw my cap. And maybe it was a kind of betrayal: of what we had going, of our silent agreement to endure together. Of something else between us, still unspoken.

"Don't worry," I said, stepping toward her. "I'll convince him to let me wear it."

"How are you planning to do that?"

"I'll figure it out," I told her. Then I added quietly, moving closer, "Sweet talk and dirty talk are the same with him, I'm guessing."

She rolled her eyes. "You're kidding me, right?"

I still wasn't sure why she was upset. But at least she was paying attention. Maybe it meant she cared. I felt bolder. I lingered there, near enough to breathe her in, her scent like what I imagined mornings could be.

Claudia took a step closer. Eyes on me, she ran the fingers of her right hand once along the brim of my cap. Then, glancing toward the door of the kitchen to check if anyone was coming in, she lifted the brim, bent over a little, and kissed my cheek.

It felt as though she was saying goodbye, and I would need to convince her otherwise. But before I could try, the door swung open, and one of the cooks strode in, coffee in hand.

"Ladies," he said in greeting, and went to hang up his jacket in the closet.

We shuffled away to start the morning prep.

◇

Eventually, Claudia ended up cutting her own hair so short she'd have no reason to use a hairnet either.

The manager left her alone after that, though I wondered again if the job would be hers for much longer.

"You're lucky he doesn't have a thing for tomboys," I said to her, winking, as we stood at the six-burner stove.

We were frying eggs and bacon, and the scent and the heat from the pans coated our skin.

She leaned closer to me.

CLAUDIA

We shared our breaks together, Eva and me, out back behind the diner.

One afternoon, in the chill November air that always makes me think of taking shelter, I mentioned I was grateful for the steady work.

Eva reached into her pocket for another cigarette. "You really think this job is something you need?" she said. "You're a fool."

"Sorry."

She took her time while she lit up. "Why do you apologize so often?" She glared at me, blowing smoke. "You're not queen of the world. You're not so important everybody thinks you're to blame."

We rested against the brick wall in the shadows under the fire escape, shifting our weight from one tired foot to the other. My thoughts turned in tight circles. Something urgent about Eva always made me feel both so wide and so narrow.

"Don't settle for this," she said, looking around, as if her attention was drawn to something more important.

I couldn't stop watching her.

Eva took off her baseball cap, and her muddy red curls came loose from the clasp where she'd tied them back. They fell around her face like a tattered wreath and tangled with the blue bandana knotted at the divot of her collarbone, the one she used to wipe her face in the heat of the kitchen.

What did life taste like to her? I wondered.

She looked back at me, and I quickly dropped my gaze—first to my old shoes, then to the cigarette I dropped to the ground and covered with the weight of my heel, then to the brick wall a few feet away from where we stood, pocked and lined with grit and dust. I tucked both my hands into the pockets of my jeans so she wouldn't see how they were shaking, but then Eva leaned in and let me put my arms around her instead.

There's a thin scar running halfway across my cheek that I got as a kid, from falling in a race. An ordinary mark I used to imagine as evidence of a battle. Eva reached up to touch it with the edge of her tongue, softly, just tenderly enough to be almost more than I thought I was ready for.

◊

Most of the things I learned about Eva were things I wasn't expecting. Mostly, she just kept me guessing.

Only after a year in the kitchen did I find out she was already planning her getaway. "If we just worked here part time, to pay for something like college," she said, "it would be different."

I didn't really know what that difference meant. High school was all I thought I'd be able to get. This job was all I needed because it was all I knew I could do.

But Eva had me dreaming wild. I began to think about going to George Brown, to become a chef in a serious kitchen. I even considered applying for a student loan. I knew debt could be a trap, but I was caught by how much Eva wanted something more, by the need she had to go.

I gave her my charm bracelet for her birthday that year.

Each of the little planets in our solar system hooked to its links, metal flawed from miniature half molds, the sharp clasp rubbing blue veins I saw pressed against her skin when she turned the inside of her wrist toward me. Each part of the dangling universe painted silver and gold, shivering in the air, swinging in her clipped shotgun salutation, casual, knees and arms blossoming bruises, bad-luck violet.

How hungry we were then. A storm of coffee and nicotine on her lips and mine, only eating enough when we were working. Taking something here and there on the side, the pies we divided to devour. Our hands touching underneath the table on lunch breaks we now spent in the sticky vinyl-seated booth at the very back of the dining room. Hauling ourselves up to work again, heated by the kitchen. Ringing the cutlery in the big wash bins as if we were trailing a flurry of wings of knives and forks, to drown out the sound of that world, get liftoff.

At night, I studied the ragged rash around the tattoo across her hip as if it were a book, new ink injected into tender skin. What I wanted badly enough, I was just beginning to understand.

◇

I thought I could handle being in that kitchen. It helped that you don't have to be pretty there, don't have to serve yourself up. The pay is regular so you keep going, and eventually you get faster and more able. Sooner or later, there's less treading water, less threat of being pulled under.

It helped that Eva was there. That I could come through the haze of every single early morning and find her, the sharp scent of smoke and stolen cologne on her skin—that was what kept me buoyant, working and waiting.

We started sharing apartments, moving all over the east end with our cat, Trout. I called him that for my love of contradictions. We lived on streets named after trees that I would go look up at the public library. "To match a name to a face," I explained to Eva, stoned, when she asked me why. "It's like in our apartment, we're living in the trees' organs. Along their veins. The curvature of their particular branches, the shapes of their specific leaves."

"Are you studying to be a biologist now, a treeologist? A fucking poet?" she replied, laughing. Then she paused. "We should cover this ceiling with a mural of trees. I've always wanted to do that in a room. We'll steal some paint from somewhere, and brushes. I had good ones back in high school." She grinned. "I didn't know how rich I was back then."

We would walk around at night, going nowhere in particular, dreaming to somewhere, turning the streets away. Passing through neighbourhoods slammed with action, accidents, heavy voices, whistles in the dead of night, bone-dry pavement, blood on the sidewalk. Hotel facades, burned-out institutions, social services with their seams showing, spilling out, broken storefronts descending, apartments towering overhead, uncertain shelters fought for and stolen.

We kept moving as if we could choose the chase.

"This is not enough for us," Eva told me once, pointing everywhere. "It's time to make a change."

Neither of us believed in fate. What happens is not for any reason other than the things you do and the choices you make. You can't rely on what should or could be.

◇

In our second year together, we were living in a third-floor attic apartment. The radiators there didn't churn out enough heat in the winter. Then the cheque for my share of the rent bounced, and I knew we couldn't call the landlord to ask again about fixing the radiators. It got cold enough that we could almost see the plumes of our breath. We were both shivering.

The bounced cheque startled me because I'd just borrowed some money from an acquaintance, a guy named Darren, to help pay for my share of the phone bill. I'd thought it'd be enough to also cover a college application to George Brown —which was going to be a surprise—and to buy wine and weed to help us through the cold.

It wasn't. I'd been so focused on the future that I lost track of the exact costs in the present.

I didn't know how to tell Eva about the missed rent. Nor did I know what to say about Darren. How he suddenly wanted me to pay back all of what I owed him, sooner than we'd agreed. How the abruptness of his demand made me uneasy. How he knew where we lived, because he'd looked up our address in the phone book. How he might be coming for me any time now, maybe even that night.

So when she mentioned the cold, I said to her: "At least there's no one living above us. And we can almost see the lake from our window in the kitchen."

"You can't see anything over that brick wall next door." She rubbed her hands together to warm them and pulled at her collar.

"Do you want my scarf?"

"No. You wear it." She turned away. "We should've

known there was a catch to getting this place so cheap."

I shrugged, let the old wool hang loose around my neck, and stuck my hands into the front pockets of my coat. The cold was seeping into the joints of my knees and wrists and around my feet, like shoes that fit too tight.

"I'll try calling about the heat again tomorrow," I said, wishing it could be true.

"Our phone isn't working either," she answered, shaking her head, looking angrier than before.

That was when I realized Eva hadn't paid our phone bill yet, even though I'd already given her my share of it.

I decided that I wasn't going to tell her about the cheque after all.

Nervous, I rested my hands on the edge of the table's firm, flat surface for balance. My library books were stacked there neatly in a pile because I didn't have the shelves for them yet—the ones I was planning to build. I looked down at the books. Science fiction and fantasy, chef biographies. I counted ten of them.

"Any idea what's wrong with the phone?" I asked.

"Why do you read all this crap if you can't actually say what you're thinking?" Her voice jarred my silent counting, shook up the sediment of dread I felt and dragged me through it. She picked up two of the books, one in each hand, and threw them hard across the room. They opened like accordions in flight and hit the wall behind me.

Stunned, I flinched but refused to move. I felt a familiar sense of being boxed in, being caught up in something beyond my control. I counted the seconds of silence.

One. Two. Three.

I saw her reach for more of the books, and I knew I had to leave the room.

EVA

All I wanted was a little peace. Everything was going wrong at once.

When Claudia left, I sat down on the floor and cried. Then I called to her. But she didn't reply, didn't come to me.

If it hadn't been so cold, I would've even offered to help build shelves for all the books she thought she wanted. Eventually, I picked up the ones I'd thrown, smoothing the pages.

At work the next day, we moved in wide circles around each other. I left early without letting her or anyone else know. I didn't care. I was almost done with that place anyway. The city was smothering me, smashing me up so I couldn't think straight. I knew it was time to go.

But what about Claudia? Should I try to take her along? Would she even join me?

She was starting to seem like a mystery again, like she had in the beginning. As if she was turning away from me.

Bundled in my hat and scarf, I walked and walked, watching the snow blanket the pavement around me, getting blinded by it. So cold, though I was moving fast, because my feet were soaked from the holes in my boots.

When I got home that evening, Claudia was the one acting like she had done something wrong. Her books were gone.

Why was she pretending like she'd forgotten what I'd done? It scared me.

She said hello and smiled, the same sudden smile I'd caught in the mirror the first time she walked into the diner. Self-assured and hungry. But also calm—that gorgeous calm of hers, though now I knew about the ripples underneath. Her calm always rattled me, kept me from knowing which way to move. This time it stopped me from apologizing right away, like I'd planned.

We propped open the door to the outer hallway to let the heat from downstairs seep in. I kept an eye on the entrance, listening for footsteps, and I noticed that Claudia did too. We were not new to the present danger of strangers—strangers, and acquaintances, there was always a question of who could turn against you. But for now, there was only the binding force of the deep cold.

We opened a bottle of wine. Red, sweet, and cheap, the second of two she'd brought home a few days ago. I felt it thick at the back of my throat, a floating red carpet lifting me off my feet. This was some sad goodbye party.

The layers I'd put on for warmth felt ribbed and ruffled. I didn't like the stifled, swollen feeling, and I kept trying to smooth down my hair and my clothes. I was worried she was going to ask again about the phone, still useless on the table in the corner.

We shivered in silence. Claudia seemed lost in her own thoughts. She looked at the floor.

"Why can't you just be direct for once?" I demanded, trying to catch her eyes. I could hear the burn in my own voice, the way it hurt, the way it gave me some force.

Claudia seemed more resigned than surprised when she finally looked at me.

I was breathing fast. My chest hurt. Everything was moving fast, making me panic.

She still wasn't saying anything, so I decided to make a show of looking for the money for the phone bill. That was the issue here, wasn't it? She was mad about the phone, but she wouldn't say it to my face.

The truth was, I'd kept the money she'd given me to pay the bill. With it, plus my next paycheck, I was hoping to pay back a debt I owed to my friend Jackie. I'd borrowed from her a while ago to get things I thought I needed at the time, but I could hardly remember what they were. It would have been a huge relief, not owing anyone anything. Then I could focus on the phone bill, focus on the future. Mine and Claudia's.

But what did it even matter now? Why should I tell Claudia anything?

It was always me doing the telling, not the other way around.

Claudia hadn't moved at all. I could feel her eyes stuck on me. All I wished for in that moment was a reaction from her, a way out or a way to reach her. And it made me frantic.

I picked my purse up from where it lay on the table and turned to her. As I did, the purse fell open and my things spilled onto the floor and rolled underfoot. The only money in there was some loose change. Exactly three dollars and twenty-two cents in quarters and dimes and pennies. I'd counted it earlier.

As we watched the coins come to a stop, I got angry again, as if the heat of my anger would fuel me through the long cold night.

But still, Claudia said nothing.

"I'll tell you what I think then, if you're just going to sit there," I said. I took a breath. "I think you don't say what you mean, and you don't mean what you say. You always leave me guessing. I think you're a liar."

We glared at each other.

"Sometimes, I wish you'd just shut your fucking mouth," Claudia said quietly, every word a hard smack.

The space around us felt closed and tight. I couldn't focus long enough to figure out how to make it right, to rearrange the order of events.

We had swung our wrecking balls. I was afraid.

Claudia got down on the floor and began picking up the scattered contents of my purse. The idea of my possessions in her hands was strangely soothing. But she gave them all back to me quickly, like it hurt to hold them.

I decided now was the time to go, before she had a chance to ask me to leave. I would not be thrown away. "I'll see you," I said, then moved so fast I didn't even hear her close the door.

CLAUDIA

When Eva was gone, I got back down on the floor.

Trout was hiding under the couch, sitting in the shadows with his eyes like glass reflectors, each catching the light, his nose raised alert, as if he could sense the danger I felt in the air.

I thought about whether Eva still wanted me. Not much, not anymore.

If Darren showed up, I could only promise him that his money was coming in a couple of days. That's all I could tell him. But I hated to lie. That wasn't me.

It was so cold with the door closed and locked again. I turned on the stove and boiled water in the kettle. I thought I'd need instant coffee to stay awake, but in the end, it was thinking of her that kept me up.

"C'mon, Eva," I repeated to myself, like a harsh kind of prayer, punctuated with the sound of my fist on the table.

What would I say to her if she was here? But words could be explosions, so I swallowed them all, shoved them to the back of my skull, the aching there. Anger. It won't stay there for long. Like oil, it splatters everywhere if you're not careful. It's a shapeshifter. I used to mistake it for love. Whatever went flying, whatever broke, whatever got raised and brought down hard like a curse, I used to confuse it all with love. I thought I'd learned to understand the difference, but maybe not. Could Eva? I wasn't sure she knew how either.

Where would she go in the middle of a winter night? What was she doing to me?

I looked at the phone that wasn't working. I went into the kitchen, checked the weak latch on the window, closed the curtain. Someone could still easily get in that way by climbing up the fire escape. My heart was racing. I knew I couldn't last the rest of the night in the apartment without Eva. It was dangerous here without her.

I packed a suitcase, then dragged Trout out from under the couch, his claws scratching in protest, and scooped him into his carrying case. Before I left, I wrote Eva a note in red marker and put it on the kitchen table. *Someone's looking for me. Be careful. I've got to go. I have Trout.* Finally, with the last twenty bucks I had in my pocket, I took a cab to our friend Jackie's in Parkdale.

Part of me hoped that was where Eva had gone. That she was already there.

◊

When I showed up for work the next day, Eva wasn't in the kitchen.

I asked the manager if he'd heard from her.

He shook his head, refusing to look at my tired eyes with his. "No more," he said, walking away.

"Sorry?"

"I don't pay her to get sick," he hollered from across the room. "She's done here. That's it."

"I'm sure she'll be back tomorrow. Our phone isn't working so she couldn't let you know she needed to take today off. I think she's really not feeling well."

"No, no, she's done here. And you are too if I catch any more messing around."

After all the time we'd spent there. All the work.

I'd put the time in, did things right, and it was still ruined.

What Eva and I had together, in that kitchen. Just more wreckage to remember.

At first, my curses came out hoarse, and got swallowed up by the clamour of the kitchen. I picked up my bag and moved toward the back door, and I shouted at him. I wanted him to hear. All my anger, everything. I turned on him.

He walked around the counter and looked at me in disbelief, shaking his head.

"Who do you think you're talking to? Are you out of your mind? Stupid kid. Get out of here before I call the cops."

When I saw the fists he was making with his hands, I thought of fighting him. Anger wrapped its arms around me, oil and fire. But I shook it off, and left before he could approach me.

◊

I wondered about going by the apartment to see if Eva was home, but the thought made me feel hollow. I was still worried about running into Darren. So I stayed at Jackie's and waited. But a whole week went by, and there was no sign of Eva. No message, no call. When I finally got the nerve to dial our number, the phone line was still disconnected.

That was when I knew she was gone.

"It kills me," Eva used to tease, "how you move so slow and quiet."

I told myself that I wasn't going to get dragged down by her longer. That I wasn't going to lose myself. I needed to leave it all alone. I needed to contain the weight of it.

◊

I still walk the old neighbourhood on my way to my new job. I'm in a bigger kitchen now. It moves faster, with more of a system, and there are more rules I can't afford to break. But I can find my way around another place without much difficulty. They'll see how I can cook.

Winter is finally over. Later, in the spring, I'm going to start taking courses at George Brown. They decided to let me in after all. The loan I'll get for tuition stretches out around me like a strange new city.

Everywhere, there's something of me spent, something owed.

Sometimes, I wonder if I'll see her again. In the back seat of a cab, the window rolled down for the feeling of flight, or on a bicycle at night, strains of light rushing past as if to race the shadows sliding faster below. One of us always on a corner, the other one flying by.

If I do see her, I'll stay silent as ever, until she's gone, down the sheer halls of the empty streets.

We both do what we can to be safe.

CAPTIVE SPACES

HER SHIFT BEGINS IN THE MIDDLE OF THE AFTERNOON RUSH HOUR. Stepping from the gaping mouth of the subway station, Jackie blinks in the sun. The sidewalks are full of office workers who stream from buildings onto the street, drifting and charging past her toward the tunnels and trains, or pooling above ground at streetcar and bus stops.

She checks her watch to see she's running out of time, then plunges into the steady current of people. She wants to move as if she belongs in these tall city corridors, between the massive office towers of steel and glass, despite the sense they could swallow her whole.

Jackie looks up, watching the bright reflection of the setting sun shattering the looming walls of glass into shards of light. Shielding her eyes, she glances further to the sky for relief. It's a closed window, growing smaller, eclipsed by the strain and grace of the buildings' height.

She tries to focus on what is in front of her, the street to cross, but it keeps changing, rewritten again and again by traffic. *Claudia*, she thinks. *Picture her.*

Claudia's here, downtown, somewhere, settling into her work for the evening. Her white sleeves rolled halfway up around the edges of her tattoos, stars, moons, the line *no one's above us, just the sky* on the inside of her right forearm. Wielding a glinting knife in a bright kitchen beside the cavernous dining room at the base of one of these office buildings, she begins to create elaborate meals.

◇

Claudia told Jackie that she has more freedom now than ever before to make what she wants, as long as it fits within the restaurant's concept. But instead of explaining what that concept was, she began to walk out of the room.

That's how it goes with Claudia: she'll start to say something that seems important and leave the rest for you to figure out yourself. Jackie thinks Claudia is more interested in the process of coming up with an idea than the result. She wonders if it's because Claudia takes answers for granted, as if they don't need to be spoken, nailed down, to be understood.

Before Claudia could leave, Jackie asked her what she meant by the restaurant's concept. Claudia stopped in the doorway, filling it with her height, and said: "Meals without history."

"How is that possible?" Jackie asked. "What does it mean?"

"Anything you want it to," Claudia answered, as though the question did not surprise her. "The idea is that the food—the way it comes together as a meal on a plate—is different from anything you've tasted before."

"But how can you taste something without remembering what it is or what it reminds you of? Doesn't everything have a history?"

Claudia nodded. "Right. But the idea is that the way the different ingredients come together is new. It's the boldness of the claim that brings customers in. It makes them wonder, just like you did now." She shrugged. "I know what you're saying. It's not my idea though. I just have to work with it—cook with it."

Claudia says it's the best place she's found in her seven-plus years of working kitchens, starting with the diner. With Eva.

Jackie had never gone into the diner. Only heard stories. *Let me tell you what the place was like.*

◊

Jackie stops at the edge of the sidewalk. She leans against a newspaper box and takes off her glasses, puts her hand across her eyes. Her thoughts are trespassers.

Always keep moving.

She starts walking again, still thinking of Claudia. Pictures her cooking over an industrial stove, the smells and stains of the kitchen that seep into the clothes she changes out of before she comes home. No trace of the kitchen, no sign of where she's been when she walks in, except when she moves closer, except on her skin.

It's dinnertime, and though she ate before leaving for work, Jackie's hungry. At Claudia's restaurant, they're probably serving bread to start, made fresh on site, still warm in a basket under a bright cloth. Below the crunch of its thick peppery crust, the bread must feel so soft, like a pillow, held and torn between the teeth. She imagines it as she darts around a car caught in the intersection and avoids a bike courier ripping around the corner before the light changes.

And the meal tonight? It would have a lot of spice, because that's one of Claudia's specialties—she always adds heat to the sauces, different layers of it. Flavour like a fire burning at the back of the tongue, lighting up the darker hollows of the mouth.

Then later, dessert. Tasting of what? Rosewater, cream, and something sweet and salt tipped.

◊

"What's on the menu tonight?" Jackie asked before she left for work. She asks this a lot, though Claudia doesn't usually want to say.

"Chef's secret," Claudia answered. She lifted her hand to mess up Jackie's carefully slicked-back hair.

Jackie saw it coming. She reached up quick to grab Claudia's wrist with her left hand, an old self-defense move, one of the first ones she was taught. Though she was out of practice, the gesture was still habit to her, body memory flooding back from years of martial arts classes taken in the corner of a dusty gym.

Claudia did not seem surprised. She smiled with her eyes only and waited, her arm still caught in Jackie's grip. Jackie didn't know what to do next. Ask about the menu again? That'd be like trying to force water from stone.

"Okay," Claudia said. "Relax. I won't touch your hair. I know it's perfect."

Jackie realized she could feel Claudia's pulse under her thumb. She released her hold.

◊

From Grade Nine until after Jackie finished high school: karate, kickboxing, punching bags, and reflex bags—but no boxing, no real contact—the blocks and punches and kicks falling in and out of rhythm with the clanking lifting and falling sounds of the weight machines.

At first there was the shock of the solid force that fighting required. Not just the physical force alone, but the delivery of it. A solid mind. The way it made her limbs stutter at first, and how out of balance she was in the fighting stances required.

But she didn't quit, because it felt like survival, and because what she did in the gym was more interesting than anything else she could think of to do, was safer than anything else she had begun to realize she wanted.

What did all those hours of training and practice, before and after school and on weekends, in exchange for helping to clean the floors and equipment in the evenings, come down to?

It meant the ground at her feet, not her face against the floor.

She practiced again and again until her body was a quick blade cutting through what real threat was left—no threat. Just ghosts, and security.

Eventually, it got her into her line of work.

Jackie began working as a guard about eight years ago. First, part-time hours at the droning, dizzying malls on the outskirts of the city. Then, the company promoted her to work downtown at big office buildings where everyone seems to have something towing them along. A year ago, she got offered a night security position at one of the big bank headquarters downtown, along with a small raise. She thought Claudia was proud of her.

But would you be surprised at where I've ended up? Did you think I had it in me?

◇

She's two blocks from work now, at the edges of the gathering dusk. A steady flow of faces and forms ripple in and out of shadow. The light still refracting off the shining metal surfaces of cars and trucks, and the polished stones of buildings, tangles with the evening, softening forms. Even the patch of concrete at her feet seems pliable, as though it would give under the weight of her step, grey cement folding inward like a sponge.

She stumbles at a curb and catches herself, nearly falling to the pavement.

Look out!

The light turns green and people brush past her. The air, when she inhales sharply, is harsh with exhaust from the cars lined up bumper to bumper, nowhere to go.

She stops again and looks around, to gather her thoughts, to calm her mind, filter what she is seeing. Tries to pretend nothing happened.

The pavement is solid again when she presses down on it hard with each foot. Testing, looking around.

As the sun goes down, the brightly lit interiors of the office buildings get easier to see from the street. Just now, there's a movement at a window six stories up. A small woman, framed by the glass, waves a pale cloth. She's looking down at the sidewalk. Is it red, the woman's hair?

Then the real question drops into Jackie's mind, like a spider from a strand of its web.

Eva?

The woman in the window turns away, flicking the cloth in her right hand as if it were a signal. She must have been cleaning the insides of the windows.

Did you see me?

I have to get to work, Jackie tells herself.

I've been waiting for you.

◊

Jackie arrives at the start of her shift with no time to spare. She shoves her bag under the security desk at the centre of the bank tower lobby and takes her position, straightening the collar of her jacket, placing her feet shoulder-width apart.

The desk dwarfs her. She thinks of it as hers sometimes, as though it belongs to her. It's long and wide, and set on a slanted gradient starting just above eye level so that she can hardly be seen when she's sitting there. The seat can only be accessed by unhooking one of the two heavy black ropes hanging between two waist-high metal posts at either end of the desk. These are her partitions.

Behind the desk are two rows of five computer screens, and an electronic door-lock system diagram lit up green in all places where the locks are functioning properly. A flashing red light means an emergency malfunction.

The walls of the lobby are clear glass from floor to ceiling on three sides, with sets of wide revolving doors on each side that she locks after dark. Behind the security desk rises the fourth wall made of massive slabs of what look like marble, a pale cream colour with flecks of grey that glint depending on the angle she takes to view its surface. It frames three sets of large copper-coloured elevators shining as if they're polished each day.

She wasn't sure how she felt about working nights at first. It messes up her sleeping pattern, and it could start to mess with her head, if she let it. But a hard run or a workout with weights after she wakes up in the afternoon wrings the weariness out of her body. Then she's ready for the night and is, for a while, clear-headed.

On the night shift, there's just the one floor she has to guard. She's mostly on her own, but that just means she only has to rely on herself. It should be enough.

◊

Before high school, before she ever stepped into the gym and learned to move, fight back, Jackie's very name held the weight of disaster.

The girls in her classes hollered it louder than anyone. "Jackie!" Like it was a crazy joke. From street corners and down hallways, dragging out each of the two syllables, their calls pitching higher as she walked away. Her name was how they'd try to cut her open and get inside.

But then she met Eva. And when Eva said her name, she made it new.

"Hey Jack," she would say in greeting, using that deliberate, even tone she had, just an inch away from fury. Insisting the name deserved to be spoken. Her eyes would meet Jackie's, hold them, even as the other girls walked past, either staring or collapsing against each other in hilarity.

"Hey Flappy Jackie. Fucking fag-girl," they'd say, like an ugly secret.

But Eva would continue, "It's good to see you." And the blades of laughter dulled.

Was it a spell?

Despite herself, Jackie wouldn't let go of Eva's eyes, not until they were gone.

◊

By eleven, the cleaners have finished, and they say a quick goodbye as Jackie locks the door behind them. One other guard is working the shift with her tonight, up in the executive office suites high above. He'll be down to give her a break at three.

Here in the lobby, the surfaces of the giant floor-to-ceiling glass walls reflect the brightly lit interior, obscuring the outer world into shadow. If Jackie looks hard, she can see the hazy glaze of streetlights, and the shine from the neighbouring buildings like massive glowing beacons in the dark. Anyone looking in can see her every move, as if she's alone on stage in an all-night performance.

Her hands shake, trying to get free of what holds them. An old dread moves, first feathery, then tight, in her chest.

Why now?

Jackie swallows hard to tame it and realizes her throat is dry. Where's her Thermos of cold tea? She reaches for her bag tucked underneath the desk, then catches a sudden movement out of the corner of her right eye. She spins around, scanning the interior, the bag swinging from its strap held tight like reins in her hands.

It's only her reflection in the wall of glass.

The cameras are recording her every movement. She tries to look in control, reaches into the bag without taking her eyes off the glass. Don't look away from your opponent. Hold their gaze, stare them down.

She finds her Thermos, opens it to take a sip, swallows, then sucks in a lungful of air.

There's more movement. On her left, to the other side of the lobby.

Jackie flinches. The liquid catches in her throat, making her cough so hard she has to lean forward to catch her breath and close her eyes for a moment.

It's only headlights, probably a night delivery to the building across the street.

That's all it is.

Eyes open again, she watches the movement turn and disappear, her heart racing.

Eva?

Listen. Now she hears a voice, or the memory of one, thrown softer, then harder, against the walls and ceilings of the bank lobby.

I haven't changed that much, Eva. As you can tell.

◊

Jackie remembers the night she first met Claudia.

Eva kept mentioning the girl she'd been seeing for a while, so Jackie was curious. The only thing she knew was that the two of them had met working at a diner together on Yonge Street, and that Eva was plotting their next move. Something new and better.

It was normal for Eva to be looking to the future. Jackie thought it was because Eva couldn't trust the present. It wasn't enough for her.

They all met at a club downtown, where the dancing was fierce, the crowd was mostly friendly, and the bar staff would serve without asking for ID. And as the three of them stood together in a triangle, Eva introduced Claudia to Jackie, shouting her name over the sound of the music.

She was tall, like Eva said she would be. Not much taller than Jackie, but enough to make an impression next to tiny Eva. Jackie's old friend and this new girl looked good together.

Jackie remembers how still Claudia stood, how it took a lot to get her to smile, and later, to move. But Eva seemed to know exactly how to coax these from her.

The music surged and pulsed. They stepped back into a semicircle to look around, and Jackie caught the eyes of a few strangers walking by. But she wasn't interested in following up those glances. She was too curious about the pull between Eva and Claudia. She could feel it, like she had discovered the strength of a force field.

"Jumping Jack," Eva said after the first round of drinks, her tone halfway between a joke and a question. "Dance for us." Then she smiled at Claudia and pulled her close.

Jumping Jack was a nickname Eva had given her back in high school. Eva revelled in telling people about themselves, showing them she could name whatever clung to them—even if it was a sore spot, something they wanted to hide. In Jackie's case, *Jumping Jack* alluded to how on edge she used to be, how she was always ready for escape.

Jackie no longer let anyone call her anything, but Eva liked to remind her of the nickname anyways. That night, maybe it was to show Jackie—to prove to her—how much they'd both changed. There they were, in the club, maybe in love. Buying their own damn drinks. Not afraid.

"Hey, Jumping Jack," Eva repeated. "I said, dance for us."

Jackie found herself turning to the crowded dancefloor. There didn't seem to be a choice. Whenever she looked back, Eva and Claudia were in each other's arms. The crazy energy between the two of them seemed to follow her, seemed to invite her to step inside of it—if she wanted to.

She hoped that they were watching her.

Afterwards, Eva and Claudia walked her home, all of them hot from the club, jackets open to the night, not feeling the cold, a little drunk. And Jackie realized, in what might've been an ordinary moment, fluid and clear as the empty night streets, that something had changed.

Eva seemed calm for the first time in years. It was like she was younger, had found a way to go back in time. Claudia, on the other hand, was looking up as if, from her height, she could see the constellations above the city's beaded atmosphere of hazy lights. Her manner somewhere between amused and patient. That was her strength, Jackie would eventually realize. Looking back, she wonders if Claudia had most of the answers even then, contained in all those books she read. The ones with the long titles and the abstract covers and the small print.

Falling a step behind, Jackie again saw Eva and Claudia in the same frame, fitting into each other. The pull between them becoming her centre too, no matter how she felt about it.

From then on, the three of them began staying out late together, crashing at each other's places, stepping over roommates or acquaintances sleeping on shared second-hand couches. Regardless of whatever it was she meant to them, it seemed like Eva and Claudia wanted her around and enjoyed her company. And the more time Jackie spent with them, the more interested she became in what was theirs.

Do you remember how it was?
All of us were scavengers then.

◇

Jackie is pacing now in the lobby. After every few steps, she pauses to gaze at the things she can and cannot see. She stands like she thinks a guard should, like she does every night: shoulders wide, back straight, arms at her side or folded across her chest.

Watching. Waiting.

When Jackie stops to listen, the empty lobby is thick with sound. The click-clack of her footsteps across the expansive marble floors. The ventilation system circulates countless whispered streams of air. Occasionally, she can hear the muffled motors of a cruising taxi sliding by, or a truck barrelling its late-night cargo through the back corridors of the financial district.

She often hears a tune, hummed softly. Eva used to hum while she worked on her paintings, back in high school. Little melodies, small refrains, old songs, colours constantly added to the space around her.

There it is again, underneath it all.

Late in the night, for a period of about an hour, each of the elevators' doors slide open a few inches. This is a mechanized system test. It takes Jackie by surprise, even though it happens every night. When it does, she checks her watch. The timing is never the same. Who decides? Which computer?

Jackie's mind begins to wander. She finds herself picturing a stranger entering, one who somehow does not set off the motion detector and manages to pry open the mechanically locked door. And as they move to face her, crossing one of the demarcated thresholds of the entrances, their image is captured on the camera from three precise angles.

Every guard has a story they tell themselves of what could be: imagined scenarios like vines across a wall, gradual and pulling.

The air in the ceiling vents flows louder.

◊

Thirteen-year-old Jackie landed with a thud on the pavement in the laneway, a block from school. She lay on her side, her cheek slapped by the cement, her body rattled with points of pain where it hit the ground. The school bag carrying her eighth-grade math textbook, wallet, and a small notebook of slow, half-done equations had fallen off her shoulder. She pulled it close, held in both arms like a lumpy shield.

This had all happened before.

If I stay still like this, will they leave me alone?

Above her, a group of other thirteen-year-olds circled, mostly girls, laughing. Beyond the mustiness of the ground, the air was full of their scent: vanilla perfume, cigarettes, and cinnamon-flavoured chewing gum.

You fell, or they tripped you as you tried to get away. Again.

All Jackie could concentrate on was the hurt.

She reached to her face. It was the place they could most easily find her shame, no mask ever thick enough or large enough to hide her.

My glasses are gone.

Down on the pavement, she was eye level with their black boots and bright sneakers. It was hard to see any distance without her glasses, but she could feel their lean storm gathering. The laneway, a shortcut to the back of the recess yard, was quiet otherwise.

Wherever she went, they followed. The thing they hated most seemed locked within her.

I can't say what it is.

She believed they might even be willing to break her open, to reveal what they couldn't stand to see. She knew what they would dare, beyond the burn of their words.

I'm afraid they're going to hurt me worse.

"Jackie?"

Her name said with such heat. She flinched.

Jackie moved her hands over the blurry ground in front of her. How could she find her glasses when she couldn't see anything properly?

There was laughter as she scrambled to try and sit up. She felt a kick from behind that landed on her left side, just below her heart. The force sent her back to the ground. A sound left her lips before she could stop it, something between the heaving of prayer and a sob of anticipation.

"Jackie?" the voice said again.

Someone else mimicked it, and giddy laughter rang in response.

Suddenly, a figure hurtled into view, almost tripping over her. It leaned into its velocity, on the edge of falling, legs bent, arms out as if hanging from the air, and let out a shriek—a weird, garbled cry of jubilation or pain, the kind of sound only a girl can make.

The crowd paused.

To them, what they were doing was just a game. It was supposed to be funny. Forcing Jackie to realize there was something wrong with her was just a way for them to deal with ordinary boredom, to slap away the constant biting embarrassments of their day, to figure out what they meant to each other.

But the interruption, the deranged sound, seemed to suddenly bring the moment into focus: its messiness, the ugly feelings.

They didn't think they could laugh at this part.

The stranger lurched toward them, howling, her fists everywhere.

They raised their arms to shove back at the girl. Pushed her hard. "How dare she. Hit her. Get her. She's crazy."

Jackie wrapped her arms over her head and tried to get up onto her knees. She felt another kick land at the centre of her ribs, not as sharp as the earlier one, but with enough impact that it slammed her back down to the ground. She rolled into a ball.

Something wet landed on her face. Don't let that be blood. But what she wiped from her cheek wasn't red. Spit from someone's mouth.

The fighting girl stood right above her now, throwing fast but messy kicks and punches. The crowd began to back off.

Someone was crying, telling Jackie she'd be in trouble.

They were fighting so near to her, Jackie could hear their heavy breathing, their feet clambering around her.

Then, from down the lane, the school bell rang, and as if the sound were a spell that could erase chaos, the space around Jackie emptied out.

But the fighting girl remained. She was breathing fast, kept turning to see if anyone was still hanging around for a fight. When she crouched down, her hands remained aloft, as though she wasn't sure where to put them with the fighting done.

"They've all left," she said. "That girl, Amanda, likes to fight me. I hate her."

Jackie tried to sit up. The whole side of her body from shoulder to waist was burning, and this girl in front of her was a blur. "My glasses."

"Hold on." The girl moved away for a minute, on her hands and knees beside the parked cars. Jackie hoped she'd leave soon.

Please let me go. Leave me alone.

The girl returned. "They were behind the front tires over there. They don't look broken." She handed the pair of glasses back, and as she did so, their hands brushed.

Jackie pulled away, as if any contact could lead to cruelty. She peered at her glasses. There was a scratch across one lens, but like the girl said, not wrecked. Once she put them back on, the world shifted into focus, and she could finally see the face in front of her in detail.

"Are you okay?" the girl asked, running her hand through her red curls, pulling them back off her face. There was swelling on her cheek, around a cut that would soon become a dark bruise. The girl's knapsack, though jostled, was still on her back, but the collar of her shirt was torn, and she held her hands in front of her as if they'd been burned, flexing her wrists and fingers, blowing on her fingertips.

"They sting," she explained, as if Jackie had asked.

There were bright colours under her nails. Paint.

She's so small. How did she scare them off? Jackie thought.

The girl seemed newly seized with urgency. "Can you sit up? We should get out of here."

Jackie looked down at her jeans and sweatshirt covered in dirt. "My side is killing me," she answered.

"Move slow, okay? I'll help you stand."

Jackie tried to raise herself, to push against gravity. She had to lean on the girl's shoulder to get up.

"Let's head to the park," the girl said, pointing down the street, and they started moving. Jackie limped from the pain in her ribs.

The girl continued to talk, hectic and casual at once. "Next time, you can't let them take you to the ground." She looked ahead and practiced a long glare that was punctuated by the open cut on her cheek, wet in the sunlight. "Because what they do to you will be a lot more bad if it comes from above."

Jackie dabbed at her forehead with the back of her hand to check for bleeding. "I was trying to get away."

"Yeah, that's hard."

"It always happens."

"You should try martial arts, like self-defense stuff. You know, karate. They teach a lot of things there. My cousin takes lessons at a gym. He showed me some of the stuff he knows, like how you have to keep your eyes at the exact same level with your attacker's eyes. I bet martial arts would be good for you."

Jackie thought of a karate movie she'd seen a few years ago in the theatre. "It seems like an almost impossibility," she said, wincing in pain, her jaw sore and her lips dry.

The girl leaned in close, her curls almost touching Jackie's face, her wide eyes blinking fast above her swollen cheek. No one got this close to Jackie anymore, not even her parents. At thirteen, she was already keeping to herself, building little bunkers of privacy wherever she could, running from one to the next. So tired, without relief, she'd even begun to imagine killing herself, if not for the fact she'd miss her little brother.

Jackie was in too much pain to pull away. Mesmerized by the girl's intimacy, she awaited the mockery that always came whenever someone got this close. She swallowed hard against the sharp ache in her chest.

The mockery did not come.

The girl laughed. "I like that. An almost impossibility."

Years later, they would still use that phrase to describe to each other the things they wanted.

The girl checked again to see if they had any followers, anyone coming back to finish the fight. "My cousin's gym is where he goes to learn the martial art moves," she continued. "He's older than us, in high school. But I'll find out what the gym is called for you."

She stopped, as if something just occurred to her.

"Do you remember me?"

Jackie didn't.

"I'm Eva. I drew your portrait in art class last week."

Remember.

Jackie took off her glasses again to wipe her eyes, and was ashamed to feel them filling up. She needed to get away.

"There's public washrooms in the park where we can get cleaned up." Eva put her left arm through Jackie's, like a rope tied tenderly, and they shuffled along while the tears slipped down Jackie's cheeks. "Does anyone know this is happening to you?'

◊

Jackie hears her friend's voice as if it is right there beside her.

She turns quickly, but no one's there.

The polished interior of the lobby shimmers at her, lit up like an exhibit in a museum. Every night, she studies the dustless, potted ferns, as if to burrow into their synthetic olive-green glow. She imagines diving into the smooth dove-coloured couches that look like they've never held a body, illuminated by pools of white on white. When she peers down the centre of the lobby, she can see the waiting elevators, closed for now. Their copper panels beam as she approaches. Nothing else moves. Then her eyes overflow, and she covers one and then the other with the back of her sleeve. Blinded.

◇

When Eva and Claudia moved in together, Jackie hung out regularly in their east-end apartment.

Sometimes she would stand in Eva and Claudia's bathroom, the door closed, trying to decide whose things belonged to who. Shea butter lotion in the cupboard: it reminded her of Claudia's quiet presence in a room, the smoothness of her hands even though her fingers were always flecked with little burns. The curly-hair shampoo on the edge of the bathtub: Eva's. Jackie opened the bottle to breathe in the scent.

Once, Jackie found herself in their bedroom, looking into a small silver enamel jewellry box with a missing lid. Inside were Eva's golden hoop earrings, beautiful ones that danced beside her face as she moved.

Eva caught her snooping. But instead of getting upset, she shushed Jackie's awkward apology and offered to lend the earrings to her. She dangled them delicately from her outstretched fingers, as if handfeeding a bird in the park. Jackie thought she saw a flash of recognition in Eva's expression then, wondered if Eva saw her differently in that moment: as someone more ambitious and wanting than she let herself appear.

"No thanks," Jackie muttered. "They're yours."

Eva smiled. "Well. Anytime." She put the earrings back inside the box, which she could not close, and steered the Jackie out of the bedroom, her right hand balanced, almost tentatively, on the middle of Jackie's back.

◊

The more time she spent with them, the more certain Jackie became that Eva and Claudia were night and day.

When she and Eva met as kids, Eva already had a kind of high-wire momentum, a sudden velocity she would never grow out of. In fact, it had only accelerated since then, with or without a destination. Eva was lucky to have painting in high school, access to space and supplies in the art room, a teacher with bright eyes who floated in and out and kept giving her work attention. In those years, Eva still had a means of survival. But after high school, after she gave up painting, she seemed more and more to be searching for somewhere to put her focus.

Claudia, on the other hand, was solid and reflective. Something always seemed to be happening under the surface. The library books stacked in the living room were all hers; Jackie would flip through the pages, searching for a way to decipher what Claudia was thinking about, memorizing the colours and images on the covers as if they were clues. All that said, Claudia wasn't shy—she could stare you down if she wanted. She just didn't need to say much, preferred to listen, to stand back and watch. Jackie told her more than once that she could've been a security guard too, if she wanted. And Claudia would always shrug, but it seemed like she didn't mind the compliment.

Back then, Jackie never saw her smile big, or laugh in an opened-up way. Never, except in Eva's company. And though Jackie would eventually learn how to get Claudia to do both, only Claudia can say whether it feels the same.

◇

Jackie remembers the last time she saw Eva. It was five years ago, in February. Eva had called her up and asked her for coffee.

"I feel like you're disappearing from me, Jack," Eva said, laughing, in response to Jackie's silence on the line. "Give me a sign."

True, it had been a long while since they'd really talked, just the two of them. The last time Jackie could remember was when Eva asked her, privately, to borrow money. Jackie lent some from the little bit of savings she'd added to her bank account. It was money she needed to get back soon— her savings were reduced to almost nothing, no buffer— and Eva still hadn't returned it.

That should have been enough for Jackie to get in touch, to follow up with her. But the truth was, it had become impossible for Jackie to be alone with her old friend. Had been that way for months.

The reason for it was difficult to face. She had to float in it for a while, her mind treading water, consuming most of the energy she had. Only after could she finally admit to herself the indisputable truth, something that she couldn't tell her friend: Jackie couldn't be alone with Eva because she wanted to be with Eva. Everywhere and nowhere at once.

How could it not have always been this way? Jackie asked herself.

I remember who you are, what you started with.

I remember the colours all over your jeans and under your nails, from painting the night before.

She remembered, from back in high school, the look on Eva's face when they leapt high, together, into and out of trouble. And a little later, older, how they'd come together to describe the different, brief lovers they'd found, each man and woman. Always coming back to each other.

Eva, she realized, was the only person who, in greeting or in goodbyes, would wrap her arms around Jackie like she was climbing the side of a mountain. And yet somehow, there would still be so much room to breathe, as if the act of closing the space between them opened up so much more.

How could she not have noticed before the details of how Eva's body felt against her in those embraces, humming and loose? Not have noticed Eva's hair and skin and scent spread across her shoulders? How Eva would, with one arm still reaching round Jackie, lean back to look into her eyes? How Eva would then pull closer, as if her life depended on it?

And now that Jackie understood what it was to be held in Eva's arms, she wanted it more. She could not deny it, even if Claudia was standing there watching, meeting her eyes.

Which was why—despite her better judgment, and despite it being her only day off that week to do anything beyond eating or sleeping—Jackie had agreed to meet with Eva. Only for Eva would she carve out this time from the small plot that her life outside of work had become.

The cafe was crowded that afternoon with people looking for respite from the cold. Around the wide room, the windows were fogged up. Jackie watched the steam rise from Eva's cup, found herself looking at Eva's bare arms on the table between them. Light glanced off the rim of a glass where Eva's lips touched, off the inclines of spoons, off the crystal granules of sugar Jackie wiped away, palm down so they stuck to her skin, off the pockmarked wooden tabletop she rubbed at with her thumb. Words hovered, adrift, between them. Maybe they were both unsettled from the frozen winter afternoon, shot through by the sun, sitting there waiting for somewhere new to land.

"How's the new job going?" Eva asked.

"Good," Jackie answered proudly. "Full time for six months." She said it like a promise.

"You look happy," Eva told her, and smiled.

Her smile—Jackie thought she'd seen it every single way. She knew that this time it was a smoke signal, not a reflection of how Eva actually felt.

Just what were they doing there, alone together, without Claudia?

Jackie asked, "How's it going at the diner?"

Eva laughed, a short howl that startled the older woman sitting alone at the table next to them. The woman peered over her newspaper, fingers catching at the black-and-white headlines.

"I think I'll be quitting soon. I've got to try for something else. You know how it gets when you're ready for a change. I need it."

Was she speaking of more than her job? Jackie wondered.

"Please don't tell Claudia. I haven't talked to her about leaving the city yet."

Leaving the city.

The words felt abrupt, almost violent. A hit that hadn't landed yet.

Jackie stared. It felt like they were standing together in an apartment with all the furniture removed, empty and waiting. Just the two of them, fumbling back to where they'd started, back through all the times they could have disappeared from each other—but didn't, despite the odds.

It had always been hard to say who needed who more.

"This place," Eva continued, stretching out her arms, "all of this fucking city in winter gets me down." Her small hands hung in the air, fingers spread as if conducting light.

Jackie fixed her gaze on Eva's hands, so as to not catch her eyes and possibly betray herself. But maybe that was what Eva had been waiting for—to see if Jackie had learned to fight. If she had figured out yet what she was fighting for.

Did you find the answer?

The charm bracelet on Eva's wrist, a gift from Claudia, slid down her raised arm.

"Where could you even go?" Jackie wondered, as she asked, if it was a mistake to do so.

Without me, where could you go?

"What kind of question is that?" Eva brought her hands back to the table.

"I don't doubt you'll be okay. I have no reason to doubt you. I've known you for so long." She looked away, then back, laughed reluctantly. "And you know me better than I know myself."

Eva did not smile. "That's probably true."

"It's just," Jackie tried, "I mean, we're in this together."

"In what together?"

I'm in this with you. What this is, what we have, it's becoming everything to me.

But of course she couldn't say that. It might ruin everything. Jackie searched for something else between them she could call upon—anything—so that she would not have to say exactly what she felt. "I've got to get that money back I loaned you, soon," she said, almost like a pronouncement— one that made her cringe, one that hurt to admit. This was not the language of love. But maybe it would be enough to get Eva to stay.

"Oh." Eva sat there for a minute, thinking and still. She seemed almost bewildered, too caught up in her own head-long flight to see this coming. And now she was tangled up in it, pulled tight to a breaking point.

Jackie couldn't recall ever seeing Eva in that state. She didn't dare to move until her friend did first.

Eva shook her head. "I don't have it yet. I know I said I would give it back a long time ago. I'm so sorry. I'll have to send it to you."

There was something pleading in Eva's voice. It made Jackie even more uneasy, so she tried again. Another deflection, a wider range of maneuvers. Block before strike. Defense before offense. She was starting to get fed up with herself, and this conversation. All the shadow boxing. This was not what she wanted. "You should talk to Claudia about this. I mean, she's going with you, right?"

Eva paused then, and looked right at her. For a moment, Jackie found it almost impossible to breathe.

An almost impossibility.

"What are you trying to find, Eva?" she finally asked, shaking. It was both an offer and a challenge.

Let me give you what you need.

Eva shook her head. She took her sweater from where it was hanging at the back of her chair, pulled it down over her head and chest. Jackie watched the delicate spaces tracing her collarbone, watched her shoulders pulling to tear against the blue. Her red hair clung to the fabric, tussled, alive and electric around her face. There was a darker strand across her forehead. Jackie thought of reaching over and lifting it away from her eyes, tucking it gently behind the curve of Eva's left ear with its little stubs of silver, and letting her hand linger there on the softness of Eva's cheek.

"I'll get the money back to you as soon as I'm settled," Eva said. "I promise."

Then she was up.

Jackie stood too. "Maybe you can start painting again. Remember how you loved it?" She wanted to remind Eva of a point in her life before she decided to leave, before she even thought about doing so.

Let me give you what I scavenged for.

"I just wanted you to know," Eva answered.

They put their arms around each other with the force of a heartbeat. Jackie could smell Claudia's lotion in Eva's hair as it brushed against her cheek.

See you soon?

Jackie watched her leave. And as the door of the café closed, all she could think about was how the soles of her winter boots were almost gone. How the cuffs on her coat were fraying so badly that she had to keep rolling and rolling the sleeves. How she'd already had to re-sew the seams at the shoulders where they were starting to split. How much she could've really used the money Eva owed her.

How much she needed something that was slipping away.

◇

At least Eva had chosen to go. Choosing to go is different from going missing.

How much did Claudia know?

A week after the coffee shop, Claudia showed up at Jackie's apartment. She stood at the door, holding a couple of duffle bags, and the cat in a carrier. She'd never looked so tired.

"Is Eva here?"

Jackie shook her head. "No. Is she alright?"

Claudia didn't answer.

They carried the bags upstairs, then let Trout out of the carrier. Right away, he hid under the couch.

Claudia took her boots off in the hallway, throwing off the cold night air that still clung to her coat. She came back inside and took a deep breath. "We had a fight, and Eva left," she said, focusing on the floor.

Jackie waited.

"Someone was after us. Me. For some money. Not a lot. But I don't have it right now. I got afraid. So I packed up and left too. Eva knows where I would go." Claudia paused, then added, "I left her a note to be careful, but I'm worried."

"In case the person shows up?"

"Yeah. Eva knows how to look after herself. If he comes by, she'll tell him I'm gone. But still. I don't want her to be alone there. I don't want to be there by myself."

She started to cry.

"You can stay here, "Jackie said. "Don't worry. Stay the night."

The apartment was the first one-bedroom Jackie ever rented. It was warm and familiar, with the fridge humming in the corner, and the sounds of television flickering soft, then loud, from the apartment upstairs seeping down through the floor. There was space enough for a little privacy, for two people at least.

But it was also true that Jackie had let the place go, so gradually that she barely noticed. Her things overflowed like water from shelves and drawers, poured over a collection of second-hand furniture from Goodwill and from the street. Her bedroom, too, was afloat with small and mismatched items lying around the periphery of her bed.

Boxes still unpacked after all this time, boxes for the things there were no rooms for.

But Claudia didn't seem to notice the state of the apartment. Not that night, or the next one, or all the nights afterwards.

Jackie found a clean towel in the hall closet and handed it to Claudia. "You've got to run the left tap in the shower for a while in order for the heat to come," she instructed. "Then the temperature gets hot real fast, so be careful."

Claudia nodded, as if listening to more than just Jackie's voice—as if there was another register to be aware of, playing above or wrapped around her words. A delay in transmission between them, the present being preempted by something else.

This is how all their conversations have gone ever since.

The next morning, after being up most of the night with her guest, Jackie slept in too long. She got up, showered quickly, and put on her guard uniform.

Claudia was already awake. She sat in the kitchen by the window, pulling herself together over a cup of coffee. Her eyes were swollen and bleary from crying. Out the window, the street was covered with new snow that had fallen overnight. Its pale cold glow in the morning light filled the kitchen.

Jackie went over to Claudia and held her. She did so without deliberating.

Those first few days, it seemed to Jackie like they each were living wild by their own different laws of survival. The question of Eva swung around them, ushering in a fog, leaving them searching blindly for a release, only to come across the sudden fact of her absence sprung open like something sharp, a live wire.

But then Jackie began coming back to the apartment after work to find Claudia making dinner. The smell of cooking made it feel like a home, rather than just a place to stay. They would eat, and watch some TV, and Jackie would try not to talk about what she'd been thinking about all day.

Was she going to have to lie to Claudia? To not tell her that she knew Eva had been planning to leave?

But Jackie fell into that concealment too, the same way she'd first fallen into love.

◊

It took about two weeks for Claudia to find a job in another, bigger kitchen. It was a little farther south than the diner and mostly served office workers, the nine to fivers. It was just a daytime dishwasher position, a step down from the cooking she'd ended up doing at the diner, but pretty soon, they were asking her to do the prep for breakfast and lunch.

The day she was promoted, she came home, triumphantly kicked off her sneakers in the hallway, and told Jackie she got the job.

Jackie congratulated her. "I'm glad our work shifts will line up so we can still have the evenings together," she said.

Another week went by. A letter arrived, addressed to Jackie. Inside was a cheque, folded inside a piece of lined paper. It was the money Eva had owed her. One word was written on the paper, in pencil: *Thanks.*

Jackie put the letter in her drawer. Then she convinced Claudia to check out the old apartment, to see if Eva had gone back. "If you're worried, I can wear my security uniform," she said.

The locks hadn't been changed but the hydro and heat

were off. How cold it was in those empty rooms. What they'd had on the walls had been ripped off. The cupboards were open and bare. There was a chair with a broken leg lying on its side, but the rest of the furniture was gone. It was like the aftermath of a storm, with all the debris blown away. There was nothing left of Eva and Claudia there.

It must have been the landlord. This was not something Eva could have done.

"I don't think I recognize that chair," Claudia said, pointing to the only thing left.

It was the first time Jackie heard her voice tremble. She realized, at that moment, how lucky Claudia was that she got out when she did.

◊

For weeks after Claudia moved in, she had nightmares in her sleep. She'd call out in the dark, her voice rising, a worried singing.

Jackie came to expect this. She would climb onto the couch where Claudia was sleeping and shake her shoulder gently, whispering her name. There she was, nobody's girlfriend in particular, holding Claudia in her arms most nights.

Maybe something was bound to happen between them.

She would feel Claudia's breath on her cheeks and her tears falling all over the place, on Jackie's face and chest and neck. She thought she could hear her friend's heart beating fast. Maybe it was her own.

"Thanks for waking me," Claudia would whisper, kissing the places where her tears had landed. Holding onto Jackie as if she would soon have to let go.

◊

In the early morning, when her shift finishes, Jackie rides the half-empty subway home, takes off her uniform, hangs her jacket in the crowded closet, and crawls straight into bed beside Claudia.

Woken by her feet, the cat winnows from the covers at the bottom of the bed and lands with a light thud on the carpet, like a dreaming fish splashing to the floor.

Soon, she hears Claudia stirring.

"Hey," Claudia says, sleepily.

"Hey."

"How was work?"

"Fine." Jackie yawns. "How was your night?"

"Good." Claudia stretches out a little, waking herself. "We were training some new cooks. They're young. But I think they'll do okay."

Jackie says nothing. She's still shivering from standing in an air-conditioned lobby all night.

"Everything go okay last night for you?" Claudia asks quietly.

"It was just a long shift."

She feels Claudia's right foot shaking—that small, quick vibration that takes' over when she's lying down or sitting still. Jackie had never noticed it until they became lovers. It's a sign that Claudia needs to get up and move.

The shaking stops, and Claudia turns to face her.

"I've got some good news," she says, her voice level in the dark. "I'm getting a promotion. Starting in a few weeks, I'll be one of the head chefs."

Jackie moves closer, relieved to have something good to talk about. "That's great news. You worked so hard for all this."

"I wanted to thank you especially."

"Me?" Jackie asks. "How come?"

"For being here. For sharing all this with me." She gestures around the cluttered room and its shadows.

And then Jackie finds herself in Claudia's embrace, the two of them moving together in a riot of memories.

"You too," she says, as her breathing starts to quicken.

◇

It is rare that Jackie has the night off, so she decides she will surprise Claudia with dinner, to celebrate. She goes to the market and collects red potatoes, asparagus, cold chicken wrapped in cellophane, and a hard square of butter in its thin foil wrapper, fresh basil, thyme, and garlic.

Jackie's route cuts across the big old city park near where they live. She circles along its crumbling paths, inhaling the new scent of uncovered soil tucked along the borders of old pavement. It's early April. *Around Eva's birthday*, she thinks. The snow has finally melted. What was buried is turning up, as if toward the sun. The fertile, poisonous rubble of city earth, all that's left behind by winter.

As she balances the weight of her bags, she lifts her head and notices a woman sitting on a bench. The woman is small, and her short curly hair is almost red, tossed by the wind in a swift storm around her face.

Jackie holds up her bags like sad trophies as she walks past, a solitary parade of delay and escape.

When she glances back, the woman on the bench has stood and is turning to leave.

◊

That evening, Claudia and Jackie sit on the bed together. Jackie is relieved the meal has gone well. Nothing burned or undercooked, no key ingredient missing.

She's trying to decide if she should tell Claudia what had happened at the park earlier. Claudia might want to know. But what is there to say? She saw a stranger and walked by, and then the stranger disappeared.

She takes off her glasses and rubs at her eyes for a minute. Maybe she should just go to sleep.

"You were shy when I met you," she hears Claudia say. "Quiet like you are now. I thought it meant you didn't need anyone. It made you seem tough, not easily moved. That's what made me notice you. But now I know you better." Jackie opens her eyes to see a little grin playing on Claudia's lips. "You're actually pretty soft."

"Shut up," Jackie laughs. Claudia can still make her blush.

And then Claudia replies, "You're softer than Eva."

It rings in the air for a minute, and then melts away.

Jackie is on edge. How could Claudia bring her up, as if doing so wouldn't devastate the evening? She considers pretending it doesn't matter—but letting it go is just another way of giving up a fight before it even starts. That had always been Jackie's problem from the start. Eva tried to teach her better than that.

She doesn't really know what this fight is for, but she won't let it go this time.

"I feel like I've seen her around lately," she says.

Claudia pauses, maybe surprised, and turns away a little. "I don't think so," she says, exhaling when she speaks, a low muffled laugh of disbelief.

"I do."

Claudia's voice rises a little to sound angry, unusual for her. "I think you go out looking for her, and you see what you want to see."

"Don't tell me what I do or don't see."

"Okay, fine. Where was she then?"

"In a restaurant."

Jackie was walking past an old glass storefront restaurant on Dundas Street when she thought she saw Eva standing beside a table of four, her small back to the window, her red hair longer. It was in the way she wrote nothing down as she took their orders. The swinging of her hand back and forth, just grazing her hip, dipping into her own rhythm, as she waited for them to finish detailing their appetites.

"I saw her at a bar, working maybe, or drinking there."

In the thick bright sun of a mid-Sunday afternoon, Jackie watched someone like Eva standing and smoking just outside the entrance of a place in Parkdale. She noted the way the woman turned to go back into the dimly lit room, moving as if riding a strange breeze in the humidity. She wore sunglasses, and her profile seemed angular, lean, like Eva's might be now. Silver studs peppered her ear, and her hair was held up in a struggle of red curls. The woman threw a cigarette to the ground as she went back inside. It rolled across the sidewalk, still alight. Jackie let it burn and kept walking.

"I saw her on a park bench today."

She describes what'd happened that morning, and Claudia listens, eyebrows rising, then falling, studying the bedspread, letting Jackie hear herself, the things she is actually saying.

When Jackie is done, they sit in silence for a while.

There's still a force field here that Jackie senses, but now its pull is between her and Claudia. She can feel its strength, but it's just not the same as the one she remembers so clearly from before, with Eva. This one, though sharper in its sensations, more pronounced, feels stretched thin, stretched over the past.

It's true that, half the time, with Claudia, she feels like she doesn't know herself the way she thought she did with Eva.

It's true that she's afraid she had let Eva down, and that's why they lost each other.

"You've got to give it up, Jackie," Claudia says quietly. "Let it go. Just let it go. Whatever you think you're seeing. If you want to keep moving."

Claudia puts her hands on Jackie's shoulders, her own skin scattered with those tattoos of full and crescent moons, twisted stars, lines that swirl to trace up her arms.

Jackie doesn't try to pull away. She knows what to expect, with anticipation: that familiar ache, the pull under her ribs, to be smothered by the way Claudia holds her just tight enough. A heavenly lockdown. Before she closes her eyes, Jackie glimpses the points of a star on Claudia's upper arm, flexed by the muscle running underneath it.

"What would make you feel free?" Claudia whispers, pulling her down.

Jackie says nothing, just buries her face against Claudia's neck, that smell of a lover's skin, the sustenance that she, back when she was still driving fists at a punching bag, never believed she'd find so familiar and true in another person.

What are we doing here? Is this the beginning or the end of what we want from each other.

Claudia rests her head next to Jackie's, pausing for just a minute, as if to catch her breath. Then she lifts to move her lips over Jackie's mouth, and across her cheek again, kissing her neck. Slides her hands along Jackie's body, over and under her clothes, as if searching for something to shift inside of Jackie through the different pressures of her touch.

"Tell me," Claudia says again, without hesitating. "I need to know."

◇

Jackie is sitting at the desk in the middle of the lobby again. She studies the automated security monitors, watching her own reflected expression on the screen gleam faintly back at her, the darker hole of her mouth an indistinct moving shadow. The recorded images superimposed underneath blink back as if hesitating, though via her training, she's been instructed that there's no time delay. The spaces captured by cameras from multiple angles fluctuate in quivers, seemingly caught in the force of invisible breaths. She can almost make out the whirring of tiny cameras positioned at each entrance to the building.

As she gets up to pace the lobby again, the looping mechanical sounds shrink, then amplify. Her world a cluster of noise.

OPENED FIRE

CARMEN ARRIVED HOME FROM HER FIRST TOUR IN AFGHANI-
STAN AT THE BEGINNING OF JUNE. During the three-hour
bus ride from the airport, she tried to focus on the familiar
landscape hurtling by: tall trees nestled against the sun,
pockets of deep blue water catching the light, the rusted
shine of the scrap metal yards, softly ribbed soil of farmers'
fields, the empty factories with their broken windows and
walls tattooed with graffiti. They all bled together.

When she closed her eyes, she saw clouds of flame and
heard the sound of gunfire.

Her older brother Aaron was parked outside the station
in his dark grey pickup truck when the bus pulled in. His
face lit up when he saw her. Carmen approached slowly,
waved a hand, and tried to smile. She climbed in beside him
with her single bag, and wiped at her eyes with the tattered
sleeve of her old army coat.

"That's all you got?" he asked her.

"Yeah."

"They don't leave you with much, eh?"

"I travel light."

"Good to have you home," he said.

His face, in profile, seemed a little older. The faint sketches
of lines across his temple and in the corners of his eyes made
him look like their father. Carmen wondered if she should
have been in touch more often while she was away. But he
hadn't written to her either. Maybe they had nothing to say
to each other.

"Thanks for picking me up," she said, keeping her voice strong. She ran a hand over her closely cropped hair.

Carmen sensed he had questions about why she was home, why she'd come back early. But he only spoke of the heavy rains. She turned to stare out the window.

"Worst flood in years," he said. He was talking about the river, around which their town was built. "Wrecked a lot of the places along the shore. I'm glad Mom sold her house and moved to the city before the latest storm happened. I drove by yesterday. Part of the roof came down with the force of the floodwater. We were okay though. Just a little got in downstairs. Mopped up the basement right away so it should be fine for you."

Carmen nodded. She gripped the strap of the duffel bag in her lap like it was a climbing rope and she was going up a cliff.

There were piles of ruined furniture and other flood-damaged household belongings at the end of every block as they drove along the river, heaps that her brother said just kept growing as people went about the gradual work of clearing out their property. The town didn't provide disposal bins for everyone. Empty houses lined the neighbourhood where damage from the flood was too expensive to repair.

When they arrived, her brother's wife, Melissa, wasn't there. She was on the night shift at the hospital, where she worked as a nurse.

"She's looking forward to seeing you tomorrow," Aaron said. Then he got quiet, and looked nervous, which was rare for him. "We're expecting a baby in a couple of months."

Carmen congratulated him. A new life, a way to begin again.

He offered her dinner, but she told him she was exhausted and should probably get some sleep.

Alone in the basement of her brother's house, she glanced around her new apartment. The kitchen was connected to the bedroom by a long hallway with a little bathroom at the end of it. Only two small windows, but four closets. At least there was some privacy, furniture, a door she could lock. A place to rest.

As she got ready for bed, Carmen noticed something in the air. At first, she thought the smell came from the flood damage, or maybe the mop in an empty bucket standing in the corner. But the more she breathed it in, the more she sensed it under every surface. The thin scent of burning, an aching mustiness of smoke. It clung to her body, through her clothes, on her skin, no matter how she washed. It covered her like a sheet as she lay awake in her new bed.

◊

Carmen could hardly remember life before the military. The only thing that stood out was her father's illness. He was diagnosed with lung cancer. She was seventeen.

Her father was a vet. He told her once, from his hospital bed, that he thought she'd make a good soldier. It didn't matter what else she did later on, he said—the Canadian Armed Forces was a free education and a foot in the door.

She told him she would look into it after she graduated from high school. He seemed pleased.

"I know you'll make me proud," he'd said, his eyes still bright, as he reached up to squeeze her shoulder.

When Carmen started training the next year, she felt like she belonged. She could channel her will into being a soldier, into acting the part. She wrapped herself in camouflage and grew accustomed to the genderless feeling that filled her when she wore the heavy uniform, held the weapons in her hands.

Later, she wondered if it had been a way for her to hide. In the army, there were fewer ways to meet women—there were far fewer women than men on base to begin with—and the opportunities she had, she didn't take, though they occupied her mind. The guys mostly left her alone. A couple of times, she'd needed to defend herself, in another form of combat, being on the offensive and defensive at the same time.

Soldiers are told that death is a possibility one has to accept. But as Carmen went through the months of training, she didn't think about being shot, or shooting other people. She thought only of shooting the gun. She focused only on the weapon in her hand, the targets on the range, on the movement of gear and supplies, on the presence of her fellow soldiers.

Training, for her, was about repetition and obedience, and following orders meticulously. But it was also about pushing her body as far as it would go, and discovering it could go farther. She watched action movies and imagined that she was in them, that she was becoming indestructible. Not Carmen in the uniform, but Carmen as uniform, as soldier.

In time, she came to feel that there was nothing underneath.

◇

Now that she was home, Carmen felt separate from the slow-motion routines of civilian life.

She had to force herself to leave the apartment. Every couple of days, she would go for groceries, so she could have something of her own to eat. During the warm summer evenings, while her brother was doing shift work at the factory, she would sit on the front porch with Melissa and talk about the pregnancy—Melissa was seven months along—or chat about the changes in town over the past few years.

One evening, Melissa suggested she check out the local community centre, to do something again. "Aren't sports your thing?" she asked, like she already knew the answer.

Carmen nodded, grateful for this moment of calm, as though everything was ordinary. "I guess it would be good to get out of the house," she answered.

All around them, the dusk welcomed the darkness.

"Sure," Melissa said, taking a sip of tea, watching her.

"I wonder if there's a running group," Carmen continued. "I've been finding it hard to concentrate lately, but running helps." She glanced at Melissa quickly. Had she said too much?

But no, her sister-in-law was listening to something else, laughing quietly with her head tilted to one side. "Feels like the baby is wide awake and kicking," she replied.

They sat there for a while longer, their palms against the taut skin of Melissa's round belly.

◊

Carmen's artillery unit was flying to Kandahar. Before they left, their commander told them that what they did with their time on Earth was of greater importance than how long they spent on it, that the world was watching, that their actions could change history. Carmen felt more powerful than she ever had before in her life.

"Think about where you place your trust, and pay attention to your conscience," their commander said. "Know that you are experts on the use of force and violence when necessary."

No one had addressed Carmen as an expert before. No one had spoken to her about such large responsibilities.

There was only one other woman in her platoon. The two of them tried to stick together. Jessie was a woman who came on strong in conversation, both impulsive and direct, often tripping over Carmen's shy, sly delivery. She had a buzz cut, one she'd given herself, and she convinced Carmen to do the same. Her face was small and expressive. Emotions moved like lightning across it.

One day, shortly after they met, Jessie said, "You know those fucking military ads at the bus stop and on TV, with the girls in army fatigues holding wrenches, or getting out of military helicopters? That's what brought me here."

"Did you find them?" Carmen asked her.

"Who?"

"The girls." She was half joking, half serious—maybe even flirting, if she was honest.

Jessie didn't get it, just kept icing her knee. She'd busted it earlier in the day, when one of the guys shoved her down during the outdoor drills. "I have no idea now what I would've been if I'd stayed away from this," she replied, eventually.

◊

The running group at the community centre met each morning at eight, Monday to Friday. Despite being weary from lack of sleep, Carmen tried to show up every day of the week. One of the first mornings, as she was glancing around at the small crowd, she saw a girl bending down to tighten the laces of her sneakers, her short dark hair falling across her face. When the girl stood up, Carmen noticed that she didn't make eye contact with any of the others in the group.

The dark-haired girl was there most mornings. Her name, Carmen discovered, was Aurora. Carmen thought of talking to her every morning thereafter. But running didn't exactly invite conversation. Plus, Aurora seemed to be on her own page, seemed like someone who was used to being alone and didn't mind it. She was faster than Carmen, usually at the front of the pack, her long legs kicking up and down at the earth, as if with every stride she found more reason to run, more untapped energy.

What was someone like her doing in this town?

◊

Carmen had no idea what it was like to call Afghanistan home. To grow up there, to know it intimately, the way a person knows the place of their birth even after it has been stolen from them. Packing up her old bedroom in her mother's house before leaving for her deployment, she'd found pictures of Afghanistan in old issues of *National Geographic* collected when she was a kid. Taken more than two decades ago, they depicted mountain ranges, valleys, deserts and dunes, lush orchards, rivers, jungle-like fields of wheat, opium, and marijuana. As she looked at those photos, she fantasized about learning Pashto. She wanted to understand what the people were saying to her, thought it would somehow make her less complicit in the cruelties of war.

But when she came to know the country, it was only as a soldier carrying a gun.

She kept her head down when she heard the racism directed toward Afghan people by other soldiers, pretended to ignore what they said, the same way she did when she heard them talking about queers. She was accustomed to hiding in order to get by, knew how to turn away and shrug off the words, the derision, knew how to keep her expression controlled and flat. She hoped she could rise above it—without standing up or speaking out—if she was a good enough soldier.

After a few weeks, Carmen and the other soldiers were ordered to engage in routine patrols around the villages, *outside the wire*, which meant going beyond the borders of the large basecamp and into areas where they would need to be prepared for potential combat.

Real combat, when it happened, was nothing like she'd imagined. It always happened so fast, without a chance to adjust or to reflect. Anything could happen in a breath: on the inhale, bullets fired; on the exhale, someone wounded, someone dying.

Carmen would find herself lying in the sand or behind buildings along with the other soldiers, waiting to attack invisible enemies. They would press themselves to the ground under the heavy weight of their gear, strung out with nervous energy. Some of the guys smoked, some would dry heave into the sand, some cried to themselves, the sobs digging deep in their throats, and some even started firing their weapons crazily at their own dread.

How she survived, she did not understand.

◊

Carmen finally caught up to Aurora about two weeks after finding out her name. It was near the end of a run, when they were both breathing hard, and looking ahead instead of at each other.

She only learned later that Aurora had slowed down on purpose, and had done so against her better judgment.

As they headed together along the battered shore, Carmen mumbled an introduction that was both a little out of breath and jumbled by her feet hitting the ground. She was really starting to feel the hunch of her shoulders, her upper body boxed tightly, wound up like a spring, as if she were getting ready to throw a punch.

Aurora spoke to her then. There was barely a question uttered between them—and barely an answer—but somehow they made a decision to meet, and in the brief euphoria following the run, they set up a place and time.

They'd go for drinks. That was all.

Afterwards, despite the fact that it had gone so easily, Carmen thought she had been too forward. Too obviously out of practice. Also, maybe, that she was finally losing her mind.

◊

Some of the Afghan elders who Carmen met during the combat mission insisted through their interpreters—*terps*, the soldiers called them—that the Canadian and American soldiers were as much the enemy as the Taliban. That it was their presence that caused the killing, the vandalizing of their homes, the disruption of their lives. That it was the soldiers from the West who were trapping them in the middle of a conflict in which the price even of speaking out was terrible.

The longer Carmen spent in Afghanistan, the more this reality began to crowd her thoughts. It threatened to break through the surface of what she had accepted as truth, until every step she took felt false, and every command she took direction from felt like a lie.

◊

For the first time since she'd come home, Carmen found herself sitting in a crowded bar. She pulled at the pale fabric sticking to her neck in the summer heat. She knew her T-shirt hardly fit her, but she'd rushed to get ready and the shirt was the only clean thing she could find to put on.

Carmen tried to remember where it had come from. She must have gotten it when she was smaller, maybe as far back as high school. It had been in one of the boxes her mother had left with Carmen's brother when she moved to the city. Most of what Carmen found in those boxes, she didn't recognize at first. But because she didn't have many civilian clothes left, and had no money to spend on a new wardrobe, she wore whatever she could find.

The bar continued to fill up while Carmen waited for Aurora. A group of girls sat down at a table next to hers. She hoped she didn't know any of them. Luckily, most of the people she'd gone to high school with had moved away to find work. The older folks, on the other hand, she was especially wary of. They always felt they had the right to ask questions about what had happened to her, the soldier's daughter, the fighter.

Carmen and Aurora had agreed to meet here, as opposed to any other bar in town, because it was the biggest one, and because Aurora had heard from her cousin that it was a more open kind of place.

Aaron agreed, when she'd mentioned to him that she was meeting someone there. "That's a good choice," he said, looking up from the kitchen table where he was sitting, going through the household bills. "Of the four in town, it's probably the best one. It had one of those rainbow flags in the window for a weekend in June, last year. I mean up on the Friday evening, and down by Sunday night, but still." Aaron lifted his hands, which were a lot like her own, and smiled, like he wished he could give her more.

Carmen didn't know what to say. So she waited, because it seemed like he was going to ask her a question.

"Have a good night," Aaron said, turning back to the bills on the table.

Despite all the assurances, she found she was getting some hostile second glances at the bar. She guessed it was because of her buzz cut. And this shirt—what had she been thinking when she put it on? There was a printed colour photograph on the front, of two tigers facing each other in profile, nose to nose. Below the picture were the words *Wild Cats* scrawled in a jagged black font. The sleeves were especially small at her shoulders, showing off muscles still thick from training.

Carmen tried to remember the way lifting weights made her feel: like they could prepare her for anything.

◇

One morning, Carmen and the thirty other soldiers in her platoon entered a village on foot. The sun was already tearing brightly into the sky. As she squinted through the lenses of her ballistic eyewear, she pictured herself lumbering along like a moving target, pounds of kit and a heavy net of weapons slung around her. She felt moisture on her skin, under the layers of clothing and her frag vest. Sweat dripped from her forehead and ran down her cheek like tears. Her helmet gripped her head tightly. She thought maybe she had put on the wrong one, and suddenly felt the urge to loosen it. But there was no time. She could feel her heart beating as though this was goodbye.

They had not been told the name of the village by their commander. They had not been told about the people who lived there. All they knew was that Taliban were suspected to be hiding somewhere in the village, and they were being deployed on foot to find them. If the Taliban were already gone, the task would then be to *show some force*.

"We're going to turn up there without warning. Your responsibility is to let the civilians know we're here now that the Americans have moved on," the commander said.

The soldiers around her were jittery and anxious in the heat, high on adrenaline and worn out from lack of sleep. They moved through the town toward its centre, then split into smaller groups of four or five, heading down the narrow streets past white and brown buildings. Some of the houses had been bombed by American forces and remained deserted. The unpaved streets were empty except for rubble.

Carmen closed her eyes for a moment, dizzy in the blanketing quiet and the riot of heat.

She was glad Jessie was there with her. They always looked out for each other, covertly, because anything that made you stand out from the guys could make you a target.

But she was uneasy about the small group she was with. Especially Smith, who was now positioned right beside her. He was someone she avoided. He made a game of taking jabs at her that were both aggressive and explicit, and she never knew what he would do next.

About a block away, a man stepped out of a doorway, his back to them, holding something at his side, swinging it a little as he began to walk.

"What's he got?" one soldier demanded.

"Hard to say," Smith answered. He lifted his gun. "Get his attention."

The first soldier called out, and the man on the street spun around to face them. He was too far away to make out the details of his body language or for any of them to see what he was carrying.

Smith fired a shot. The man stumbled backwards a few feet with his arms up. Then Smith shot again, and the man folded over and fell to the ground. Smith fired again. And again. And again.

Carmen flinched with each shot. She bit her bottom lip to stop herself from calling out, so hard that blood dripped down her chin and pooled under her tongue. But it was nothing like the blood the man was losing now as he lay in the street.

The rest of the group had also lifted their guns, ready for an exchange of fire. They looked from Smith to the street where the man lay and back again. No more fire came. It was quiet.

Carmen ran forward, thinking she could save the man on the ground. As she approached, a woman's screams rose up from inside the house he had come from. Someone yelled at her to get back, but she kept moving forward, and then she was close enough to see the man's eyes open, as if to watch her approach. They were brown, like her father's. Beside him was the object he had been holding. A walking stick.

There were more gunshots. Were they shooting at her now? She bent down to begin administering first aid.

Someone else called her name, a woman's voice this time, but she didn't turn around. Bandages. She needed to stop all this blood.

Suddenly, there was a heavy thud against her shoulders, knocking her off balance. She was wrestled to the ground from behind, and she fell hard with the weight of all her gear, her cheek against the dirt. She heard the woman's voice again, this time from above, pressing her into the earth.

"You better stop, Carmen." It was Jessie. She held Carmen's arms folded back behind her in a twisted embrace, and was leaning forward to speak into her ear.

"Get off of me! I'm trying to help him. He's losing so much blood," Carmen stuttered, anger threatening to split her apart.

"We're retreating." Jessie's breath was hot and fast on Carmen's face.

"What about this civilian?"

"We've got to get out of here." All of Jessie's weight pressed Carmen's shaking body down, and she held Carmen tighter. "Follow me back. If you don't, I'll lose you."

The gunfire began moving away.

"What about him?" Carmen repeated, trying to turn under Jessie's weight to look at the man where he lay silent on the ground.

"Someone'll kill you if you stay here. The other guys are losing it. I swear one of them will shoot you."

Then, without another word, she sat up, and hoisted herself off Carmen's back. On their knees and breathing heavily, they faced each other for a moment, the dust rising from their scuffle. They each stood slowly.

Carmen turned to look at the man. His eyes were still open, his face motionless.

The woman inside the house began screaming again, her voice climbing and falling in grief. As if it were a signal to retreat, Jessie and Carmen began making their way quickly back down the streets the way they'd come, until they reached a half-blasted compound on the edge of the town.

The other groups of soldiers were already there, leaning exhaustedly, cradling their guns. Carmen wiped the blood from her mouth. Her bottom lip was swelling where she'd cut it with her teeth.

The commander was telling them that they were going to head to a village farther north.

Smith caught her eye, stared at her, as if daring her to say something. He seemed angry, not afraid.

That was when Carmen started to realize that it was the beginning of the end for her. Whenever she closed her eyes, she saw the civilian's eyes watching as he lay bleeding on the ground. She couldn't shake the thought that the blood drying on her hands, where she'd tried to wipe it off her mouth, was his.

◊

The shriek of a girl with long, shiny hair at the next table brought Carmen's mind back to the bar. Her body, she realized, had tensed. She tried to open her fists and loosen her shoulders. As she did so, she heard the rattle of a semi-automatic rifle behind her. Carmen spun around and nearly knocked her beer off the table.

Nothing. Just another table, collapsed into laughter.

Carmen saw that the woman tending bar was studying her, so she turned away.

She looked down at the T-shirt pulled tight across her chest and stomach, and remembered where she originally got it from. A bargain rack at the mall in the mid-nineties. It was like every part of her life had suddenly looped backwards in time. Here she was, wearing this old T-shirt, waiting nervously to meet a girl, acting as though she'd never been a soldier, never shot a gun, never watched a bomb explode or seen dead bodies, hadn't watched her father die of an unstoppable disease.

Stop it, Carmen thought to herself. *You're just mixed up from coming home after being away for so long. You don't actually get your life back. You don't get to rewind. Don't get carried away.*

She went back to waiting, and watching.

When Aurora finally arrived, Carmen noticed a scent with a hint of flowers as she walked toward the table. It wasn't strong but it stood out from the stale, leathery smell of the bar.

Aurora was wearing something dark green and sleeveless that scooped down a little bit from her shoulders. Her arms and her neck were bare, no jewelry, no makeup it seemed.

Beautiful, Carmen thought.

Aurora slipped her hair behind her ears, but it slid back across her face again. She said hello and apologized for being a little late, to which Carmen replied instinctively, as though in greeting, that she'd just arrived herself. They paused. Then, laughing quick, Aurora apologized again, and went to order a drink at the bar.

Carmen was caught by the back of Aurora's body moving away. She looked down as if to study the amber of her beer, waiting, thinking about what she'd just seen.

Aurora returned a few minutes later, sticking her change into the pocket of her jeans, her glass clinking with ice cubes and already dripping with condensation. The ceiling fans spun fast above them, but hardly brought relief from the heat.

"Cheers," she said, raising the glass. "What a warm night. I mean I love it, but this is definitely a hot one."

Carmen nodded. *Don't talk about the weather*, she thought to herself. *Don't say any more about the weather because then it'll seem like you don't know what to say.* "So how long have you been running?" she asked, realizing how abrupt the question sounded. She tried again. "I mean, have you been running for a while?" Aurora nodded, and that question led to another, and another.

They discussed the routes the running group took, how they had changed since they first started. Carmen then mentioned that jogging had been part of her training, but that it had been on a track at the military base, all level, asphalted terrain, the route directed and prescribed between thick white lines. Nothing like the paths along the river. Those rose and fell, and you needed to really pay attention to them if you didn't want to trip yourself.

She left out all the running she had done in Afghanistan.

Aurora was staring at her, so she got quiet for a minute and decided maybe she had been talking too long. She asked about Aurora's job at the grocery store, taking another swallow of her beer.

It had progressed, Aurora told her. They'd moved her up from cashier to working behind the meat counter. She'd agreed to it because she could make a few extra dollars an hour, and because the health and safety training was free, and was something she could add to her resume. As it turned out, Aurora was pretty good at remembering her customers by first name, usually women who came in to buy for their families. They'd ask her opinion on the ground beef or pork or chicken cutlets, even though the prepared meats hardly changed from week to week. Which one did she think would be good for dinner that night? Often, they'd tell her what else they were making to go with it. And sometimes she wondered if maybe one of them would have another, better job they could offer her.

"Like what?" Carmen asked. Her first drink was done and the room was growing louder.

"That's what I've been trying to figure out," Aurora said, smiling in a way that was starting to seem recognizable to Carmen. It was the kind of smile Carmen used to see from girls who were trying to figure her out a little, and enjoying the effort—somewhere between a grin and a light invitation. Not exactly relaxed, but not fake either.

"Can I get you another one?" Carmen asked, pointing to Aurora's glass.

"Oh, sure. Thanks."

Second drinks in hand, the conversation between them continued to dance along under the pulse of the music. Carmen had to lean toward Aurora's voice. Her hearing had changed since Afghanistan. Soft sounds and anything in a higher register were muted—birdsong, for example, the rush of water, violin or saxophone. Carmen remembered how those sounds could be ecstatic and smooth at the same time, like different ways the light could shine, but they were only a lingering memory now.

She ordered a third drink, then a fourth. She rarely let herself drink too much these days, because she couldn't predict what the alcohol would trigger. But Aurora was something else—someone she never expected to find here, back home—and Carmen was desperate for something to give her a little ease, to soften her edges.

As evening pitched into the deep humidity of a July night, Carmen became more aware of the agitated tics that worried her face. Since Afghanistan, her face twitched sometimes like it belonged to someone else, and a slight stutter would seize her tongue, cutting up her words like gunfire. She ran her hands along her lips and across her eyes, trying to hide the many small spasms lurking there. But she could still feel them under her fingertips as she spoke vaguely of her time in Afghanistan.

"How're you finding it being back?" Aurora asked, watching Carmen trail her fingers across her face.

"I'm keeping myself busy. Hard to do here. As you probably know." She smiled through the tiny jerks at the edges of her mouth and eyes, wanting to distract from the lack of detail she was providing. "How do you do it?"

"All this is temporary," Aurora explained. "I needed work for the summer and my cousin has a spare room. So I'm just here for now, building a small fortune."

"Oh." Carmen said, though she meant to reply with something more, to show she was listening.

"That was a joke. Almost every cent I make is paying for my last year of school. I basically failed, spent the whole time fooling around, ran my grades into the ground. It's okay. I needed a new start. A new plan. And I like the way it is here. Pretty calm. I can lose track of myself and my bad habits here, get into the rhythm of days that don't seem to change. I can just focus on getting up and going to work. Maybe this is what I need to find some direction."

Carmen thought about how fast Aurora was able to run. She wondered if it was because Aurora had a clear picture of where she was going and where the routes ended, or if it was because she finally had the space she needed.

The DJ was starting a set. Tables and chairs were pulled aside, and Carmen and Aurora moved to the dance floor. Carmen found she could not stop blinking. She blushed in the heat, unable to think clearly, consumed with wanting to touch Aurora under the blurry lights.

"What's your name about?" Carmen asked, drunk enough now to not consider her questions before she spoke. "I mean, where did you get it?"

Aurora laughed, her eyes on Carmen the whole time. "Well, it's literally from the northern lights. You know, the aurora borealis. My parents loved them, used to go watch them when they were younger."

Carmen pictured the horizon, imagined the rippling lights' approach, and then the sound of them too, growing more powerful, deafening.

Stop, she thought to herself. *Don't lose yourself here. Don't lose what you've found now.*

"I haven't seen them," she said. "The northern lights."

She fell into the music, which replaced all other sounds. Her mind returned to feeling like it was cocooned. She was drunk, but it was okay, this muffling rescue from her thoughts.

Now, the small temporary dance floor was packed and there was so little room to move. Carmen put her hands on

Aurora, lightly, because she couldn't figure out where else to put them. She touched her arms, which felt as soft as she had imagined. Aurora lifted her arms a little and stepped in as near as she could. Carmen reached around to touch her back, which was as warm as the air pressing in around them, and rested her palms just above Aurora's hips.

"Your name is beautiful," Carmen said, relieved to finally find a word for the thought that kept coming to her mind all evening. "It's really beautiful."

When the bar closed, they went back to Carmen's basement apartment, letting themselves in the door at the side of the house so as not to wake Aaron and Melissa.

Quietly, under the dim light of an old lamp, they reached for each other, drunk on the push and pull of lust as much as on alcohol, and slipped into sex that was both furious and tender. They rolled off the old couch onto the floor, Aurora laughing a little as they hit the ground, and didn't fall asleep for hours.

A nightmare woke Carmen in the early morning. She began to weep quietly, burying her face to muffle the sound.

◊

The road mine exploded in the middle of her platoon. Carmen was thrown backward, off her feet, immersed in intense light and heat, the sound shattering inside her ears. When she opened her eyes, it felt as if she were coming up from being underwater. The air was full of smoke. She looked around slowly and saw Jessie lying on her back. One of her arms was bent underneath her body, like it no longer belonged to her. Carmen got closer, crawling on all fours in case there were more bombs, and saw that Jessie had lost consciousness and was bleeding. She pulled bandages from her bag and wrapped them around Jessie's shoulder to stop the blood. She saw another soldier moving behind the grey curtain of air, and waved him over. Together, they got Jessie across the sand, toward another soldier with a radio, who was contacting the medics located farther down the road. Then they went back for more of the injured, and for the dead.

The platoon was sent back to the temporary base. Carmen had by then lost the ability to make any sound. Her jaw was locked. She could hardly move her mouth to drink or to eat. Her tongue felt thick enough to fill up her throat.

She was given pills, but she hid them away because she knew the drugs would keep her in a haze. She'd seen that happen with other soldiers, and she wanted to stay awake and alert. Carmen didn't trust what she was doing in Afghanistan anymore, and she didn't trust anyone around her.

She decided that when her voice came back, if it ever did, she'd say something about Smith. What she'd seen him do. She knew it happened all the time in war, but to see a civilian needlessly shot right in front of her, when she could have stopped it, was unbearable. She wanted Smith to be confronted for what he had done. As if that could make up for all the wrong.

◇

Soon after her first date with Aurora, Carmen began running on her own. Every day she headed up one of the few main roads to the outskirts of town, dodging the explosions in her head. She'd scale the hills a little harder every time, maneuvering her effort into upward force. The familiar sense of speed, the jostle of her body through space, soothed her like a temporary balm.

One morning, she crouched down at the top of a hill. She was breathing hard, feeling the strain of the climb in the muscles of her legs and shoulders. Her hometown lay curled on its back in the summer heat of the valley. She pictured Aurora down there, her long hands sheathed in latex gloves, working behind the meat counter in the grocery store, tying up roasts, or preparing marinades and stuffing for the small display of take-home dinners.

Without warning, fragments of memory cut in at the edges of her mind, looping out of sequence. She couldn't tell where one ended and the other began. Her heart pounded like she was still climbing the hill. Sweat dampened the back of her neck, her hands wrapped into fists so tight the bones of her knuckles showed through her skin.

Carmen concentrated on breathing deeply to slow her heart rate. She blinked hard in the middle of the sleepy summer afternoon.

The birds and cicadas grew louder.

She stood up and swallowed gulp after gulp of cool water from the bottle she carried at her waist. Then, she walked slowly down the hill and through the streets back to the shelter of her apartment in her brother's house.

◊

Carmen's voice eventually returned. It scratched and wheezed and vibrated in her throat, but it was back.

She met with the commander and described what had happened. He did not take notes. He just looked at her.

"Why did you wait two weeks to bring this to my attention?" he asked, after a pause.

"Sir, it's been on my mind and I realized I needed to say something."

"The language you're using to describe what happened is irresponsible."

She waited for him to explain further.

"Do you understand what I'm saying?" he asked her.

She shook her head, barely.

He looked down at his desk for a moment, then back at her. "You are oversimplifying what was a complicated series of events in a high-pressure situation."

Carmen breathed deep. "No, sir, I saw what happened. There was no reason to shoot that civilian."

"But we can't know that for certain."

"Sir, I was right beside Smith. I saw and heard the same things he did. I would not have shot my gun at an unarmed civilian."

"You should understand by now that a so-called civilian doesn't equal an innocent. Not here, not at this stage."

Carmen took another deep breath. "That man should not have been killed," she told the commander. "Not that way. Not at all."

"Smith is an excellent soldier, in everyone's estimation."

"He's a killer, sir."

"Your language is unacceptable. Absolutely unacceptable. There were numerous factors in play, some of them certainly outside your understanding or control. This is the kind of urgent situation that requires firm and immediate decision making. Smith did that. He used his judgement as a soldier to quickly assess and respond to danger. He may have saved your life in the process."

"I don't think so, sir. I mean, I don't think that's true. I believe he should be held accountable for what he did, for the wrong he has done." Her voice stuttered. "That's why I'm talking to you about this. And—and that's why I refuse to work with him anymore."

The commander told her the meeting was over.

The next day, she was given a letter stating that, based on her recent behaviour, and complaints about how she'd acted in a recent deployment—specifically, her being distracted from duty during an exchange of gunfire, and resisting orders, thereby putting other soldiers' lives at risk—she was being discharged, and sent home immediately.

No longer fit to serve.

She'd failed as a soldier.

That evening, she slammed around the barracks in frustration, avoiding eye contact with her fellow soldiers. She knew she was being dismissed because they felt she might sabotage the morale of the unit. Disagreements among soldiers could cause tension and interfere with accomplishing the mission.

But what was the mission? she asked herself.

She had no answer anymore.

◇

The passage of time wasn't helping or healing her. Things seemed to be getting worse, not better. But whenever Aurora tried to ask about it, Carmen wanted only to shrug her off.

Aurora thought it might help if they got away from everything, so she suggested they go camping, at a site she'd heard about from her cousin. She would take a few days off work and they could go during the week, when there would be fewer people around.

They arrived at the site after half a day of driving, with the car stereo turned up the whole way so conversation wasn't necessary. There was a sudden new space between them that was hard to fill with small talk, even while putting up the tent together, building a campfire. Carmen moved tentatively and deliberately, the way she did any time she wasn't running, as if her body were bruised and tender.

That first evening, they mostly watched the water, getting used to each other's company, resting in the silence that comes with intimacy. Eventually they crawled into the tent together and made long, slow love, turning each other over and inside out, whispering single words again and again like prayers in the dark.

The next night, when Carmen lay down to sleep, she began to shiver uncontrollably, rattling herself loose from the darkness. Aurora held her until something opened inside Carmen, and with that release, she could act again. She reached for Aurora, tearing into her where every breath was pleasure. Their bodies led them blindly, playing each other with mercy.

Carmen slept in. She spent the afternoon on the beach, sitting on a towel, studying her hands. She wiped the sweat from her forehead with the back of her hand and stared ahead. Her eyes fluttered quickly open and shut, and her lips quivered like she anticipated getting stuck on words, had forgotten how to pronounce them, was afraid of choking on them. She felt like her heart was in her mouth, and she wanted to spit it out.

Aurora, who sat next to her on the warm sand, stood up nervously and said she was going for a swim.

Carmen nodded, swallowed hard, and turned away. But then she watched Aurora strip down to her shorts, watched her wade into the water, stepping deeper until her feet couldn't touch the bottom, watched her float on her back. She watched Aurora as long as she could, and pretended the world had disappeared.

◇

They found traces of shrapnel in Jessie's chest, so she was to be evacuated to the hospital at Kandahar Airfield.

Carmen asked to see her, despite the growing scrutiny she felt from the other soldiers. Word had spread about her own imminent departure.

Jessie lay on the bed with bandages covering her upper body from waist to neck. Her voice sounded like a rustling in the dark, requiring a huge effort to be heard above the low-level beeps and electronic pulses of the heart machine monitors, IV drips, and the muted voices of other wounded soldiers, separated only by curtains.

"They told me I have to leave," Carmen said quietly, studying her friend's face for signs of distress and finding the fear in her eyes.

Jessie didn't say anything for a minute. She struggled to clear her throat, so Carmen held a cup of water with a plastic straw to her mouth.

Jessie took a sip, then whispered, "Fine, Carmen. So leave."

"I'll write to you," Carmen said. "And we'll see each other back home."

But Jessie had fallen silent and closed her eyes. Carmen waited for her to open them again, but she didn't.

Eventually, a nurse walked by, looking at her critically.
Carmen got up and left the room.

◊

At the end of the summer, Carmen asked Aurora to move in
with her. Aurora said yes.

She was fond of coming across Aurora reading in their
apartment, or out in the backyard, which was finally dry
enough after the flood for grass to grow again. Carmen loved
the way Aurora peered at a book like it held a mystery, like
it gave her some comfort. Carmen missed that for herself.
She missed being able to concentrate on words and a make-
believe world without the memories pummelling down, without images leaping in her mind, scrambling her vision and
making her forget what she'd just read. Books and reading
were a luxury, gifts she wanted back. She wanted her life back.

Carmen began going out on her dad's old motorcycle,
one he'd left her. Whenever she did, Aurora asked her to
wear her helmet, but Carmen always ignored the request.
She'd ride around in the wind for a while, without any destination in mind, gripping the handlebars as if she could leave
and just keep going. As if it could give her escape. Ride it
into nothingness.

One day, Aurora followed Carmen into the front hallway.
"You can use the car if you want. I'm not going anywhere
while you're out," she said to Carmen.

"Nah, it's okay."

Aurora asked her again to wear the helmet. She bent
down to pick it up from where it lay on the floor underneath the coat stand, and her loose shirt fell halfway down
her back.

Carmen watched Aurora's body bending, the glimpse of bare skin. Her eyes measured Aurora's shape, as if searching for toeholds and grips to ease her body into the branches of a tree. It seemed to her that Aurora was always escaping her clothes, always slipping out of them.

Aurora brushed her hair away from her eyes and held the helmet toward Carmen. "Please?" she said. "You know the cops will pull you over if they see you riding around here without one."

Where they stood in the middle of the hallway, the odour of mold still lingered faintly. The heat of summer paradoxically seemed to make the dampness worse.

"Please," Aurora said again, the helmet in her outstretched hands, the scent of the river rising in the silent space between them.

Carmen shook her head, the tiniest gesture.

"Why not?" Aurora asked.

Carmen closed her eyes, squeezing them shut. "Right before the explosion, I was wearing a helmet about the same size. I was tightening the strap."

And then she was back there in the middle of it. She felt the helmet on her head, the sensation of the strap underneath her chin.

Stop this. You have to make it stop.

She felt nauseous. She pushed past Aurora and stumbled down the hall to the bathroom, retched painfully until it was finished, then washed out her mouth in the sink.

When she came back out, Aurora was sitting on the couch with her head in her hands. Carmen didn't know what to do, so she began to hum. She rocked on her feet for a long minute. Then she went into their bedroom and lay back on the bed, looking up at the low ceiling. She let the air whistle and hiss out of her mouth, a long, low exhalation. Just release. Her body tense and aching all over.

Aurora came in then. She sat down shakily on the bed and asked, "What happened?"

I can't make it stop, thought Carmen. *What words are there for this?*

"Carmen?" Aurora said her name like a wish.

Carmen decided she had to try again. "Sometimes it feels like everything happened there, and now I'm gone. I've disappeared."

Aurora was quiet. Two fine lines ran down the centre of her forehead, finer than the ones on the palm of her hands. Carmen had noticed them before, when Aurora was concentrating hard, or when she didn't understand something.

The last thing Carmen wanted to be was someone Aurora couldn't understand.

She looked up at the ceiling again, squinting her eyes hard to squeeze out the tears. "Everything is still happening to me, all at once, and it's still as bad as it was then, and it feels like it could end up killing me."

She shut her eyes, and she bit her lip, and there was that scar inside her mouth from when she'd cut it with her own teeth while watching Smith kill the civilian.

Aurora moved closer to her and when she spoke her voice was gentle and steady. "We need—we're going to figure this out, okay? Because this can't be—we're going to do something to help you." She reached over and touched Carmen's face gently, sliding her thumb across the wet surface of her cheeks, her temples, wherever the tears had gone. "But I need you to keep telling me about what you're going through. You can't just hold it in. That won't work."

She leaned forward over Carmen, bringing her body so near, the way she knew Carmen loved. They stayed this way for what seemed like a long time, in each other's arms, falling into their separate dreams. Outside, the streetlights came on, pouring weak pools of illumination onto the scattered piles of fallen leaves lining the road.

Later, Carmen woke from another nightmare, and heard the baby crying in the room above them. Soon, she could hear footsteps going to the crib. The sounds from above were strangely comforting to her, and she grew calmer. In a few minutes, the baby's cries quieted and then stopped, and it was silent again. Carmen's fear resurfaced, her mind dragging up images and sounds she was afraid would swallow her if she closed her eyes. Starting to panic, she turned to see that Aurora was still right next to her, fast asleep, and thought about waking her. But Carmen didn't know what to ask for, or what to tell.

Instead, she lay there in the dark with her eyes open, shaking. When she finally fell asleep it was into a dream of Aurora running beside her.

FLOOD LANDS

TWICE THAT I CAN REMEMBER, THE RIVER BLOSSOMED UP ITS INSIDES—moisture cleaving every surface, drips of water running like teeth along the edges of walls and ceilings. Afterwards, I would ride my bike, spraying up the muddy streets, my hands wrapped around the handlebars like a lover. The soaked landscape would pour by, a drowning village, a waterlogged dream.

Once, the river took our cattle, the group of them standing together in a haphazard circle, stamping their feet and shaking their heads at the wind and the rain that tunnelled round them. The river swept them all, a jangle of bodies into its rush and roll. It also washed away the birds, their great plumage going under like festival sails. It took our necessary objects: blades, beds, the fires on which we cooked. It stole the warped musical instruments bent by time and earlier floods, the scarce few photographs of children who are now old women and men far beyond recognition.

The river stole the one faded image of my great-great-aunt, Carmen. She was a warrior in her time, one who turned away from battle, into what life had left—and like me, she had no children. When she died, those who loved her named her a warrior of peace. I heard she used to ride a bike, motorized, without pedals to make it move. I have her name now, as well as my own that means song-maker and builder. But I find myself wondering if any of this matters now. Because the river will take it all away.

This last time, it took Ella's baby.

Some days, when I dream of the baby, she is laughing, other days crying. But always she is floating. Her little round legs kicking like puckery fins. Her face as visible to me as the moon.

The women crowded around Ella, weeping. And then they began to cook, spreading rich smells of food into the thickness of new moisture and the billowing clouds of insects. Nothing was dry here. Nothing was without the taste of something just gone.

They say that cries of grief bring us closer to our animal selves. I have come to believe this is true. To care for Ella is to live with a wolf or a nightingale.

They also say sadness dulls the tongue. Even so, or despite this, the women salvaged what they could from their soaked provisions. They went out further, where the waters hadn't touched, they hunted, and what they brought back they poured into their cooking for Ella's loss. I confess my tongue burned and leaped with the flavours they created, as I sat quietly, eating with my dancing mouth, and brushing away the little stabs of the mosquitoes that clung to my uncovered skin.

I ate as if I knew this food made by the grieving women would give me the strength to sleep, and it is there that I would meet Ella's baby in my dreams.

While my plate was filled and passed to me, collecting others' tears as it went from hand to hand, I watched Ella. She sat close by, but her body was in knots, her face turned away. Every bite of food carried the sensation of being alive.

Over a year ago, she had arrived in our village to take over her brother's home and care for his few cattle, while he left to find work in a larger town. She stayed a stranger to us, mostly because she was fierce about living on her own. I would glimpse her as I was riding my bike along the riverbank in the evenings. Ella lay on her side on a blanket, pillows of grass under her pregnant belly and between her legs, with an open book held close, reading it in the dying light. Seeing her there, resting intently in her weight on the ground, I almost forgot my legs turning the pedals. She had been working with the other women in the fields since the early morning, but now her body relaxed while her mind laboured and danced. How full, crowded even, she seemed, with something I imagined was pleasure.

It was not too long after this, and about five months before the flood, that Ella gave birth to her daughter.

Most people well enough to work with their bodies have left the village by now, headed for higher ground. I hear stories of what is out there, not so far away, closer to the sea—miles and miles of rusted, peeling, broken structures strewn across the land, hulking shapes like beached whales, their webbed plastic flesh torn away from their ribbed metal frames. Into the giant fruit of industry, the natural world is moving. It disassembles and it fills everything.

Whole cities have fallen, they say. Scattered leftovers, fragmented, flattened, earthbound. Only trees grow tall above us now.

I've been asked what I'm still doing here in this village half wrecked by the river, with the old people in their last days, women with young children or babies who are unable to go, and men who can't afford to leave others behind.

My name is for song-making and for building, I tell them, so that is what I'm here for.

But to myself I think, maybe there's a hidden part of me afraid to leave, and so my home will take me under with it in the end. Or else I will ride my bike until it weakens and breaks apart beneath me, and then I'll walk away. The other warriors of peace are gone. I have no family left.

For now, there's still work for me here in the village. I'm called on to do repairs, to help build and rebuild. As soon as I was old enough, but still a young girl, I started learning how to work with my hands.

Also, I can sing.

I was asked by the women to stay with Ella at night. I confess this was something new to me. My hands shook. Ella lay curled inwards on her sleeping mat, her eyes like cracks slit by pain watering down her face. All I could do was sing to her. When she shook desperately, taking raging, reluctant gulps of air, I sang. As she travelled restless through a long tunnel of haunted sleep, I sang softly, so that she knew someone was still with her.

I was never taught how to read or write. We have no paper. There are so few books left. I listen instead, and I work with my hands. Words are just sounds and the feeling of something. I can memorize stories told aloud, and I make my own songs like writing into the air. I build.

Still, there are dreams I have. Stories that take on life in my mind. In dreams, Ella lays me down and names things as she draws shapes across my body that I come to realize are letters—one letter into the next, as lips or limbs meet, until they form words as patterns of touch across my skin. Just by the lines she draws, soft and hard, fast and slow, I want to believe I could know all the words that matter to her most by feeling them, their different shapes: names of a sister and two brothers, a mother and a father, words from pages in a book she remembered, and those others she drew—maybe her children yet to come, mine and hers. But the baby's name, she never speaks aloud, even though all the time it is there inside her to be said. It is the only word I know by her touch alone, not by her voice— her mouth moving silent around the shape of a sound I cannot decipher.

Sometimes, I dream Ella is looking for the baby inside of me. She would go that deep, be gone so far below, searching, holding herself inside, that when she finally comes to surface, she is breathing hard, gasping. Sometimes, in my dreams, she doesn't know how to stop, and I can sense her diving again and again—this insistent, tender thrust of her search. Sometimes, she pulls me under too, and we search for the baby together. There, in the ebb and pull, wave after wave, when we rise, we are drenched with each other. Our bodies bearing scars, we trace and erase and retrace them.

◊

Eight months after the river stole her baby, Ella walked up behind me in the swinging heat of late afternoon. I had my bike leaning against the thick trunk of a tree and I was crouched down at its back wheel, trying to fix the chain that had come off. When I managed to pry it back on, its links would line up with the ridges of the sprocket like clenched teeth. With that solid friction between them, the chain could transfer the power from the main gear of the turning pedals to the one that propels the back wheel. This single invention of fortunate speed is one I would willingly give my entire life to.

"Never ridden one of those."

The sound of Ella's voice made me turn my head, my hands still on the slippery links clotted with muddy grit that also coated the wheels and the frame. I fingered the slackness of the busted chain, looked away and then back at her again, steadying myself.

She stepped closer and spoke again. "Never ridden one."

"A bicycle," I answered.

Ella seemed to lean limp on the air, both arms at her sides, her back straightening up against the weight of her hunched shoulders. She wiped at her face and pushed a few loose strands of hair from her eyes, the sudden motion caught by sunlight.

I looked down at her shoes, dusty and patched as these wheels I ride on. In this village, we almost religiously try to keep everything, reusing them again and again even as they fall apart.

But we possess only the tangible. What lasts in our hands makes for a slender archive. Through the scarcity of objects, how we need them. They corral us. Become something sacred. They will also abandon us to ourselves alone. I've seen them in their lank trails, floating the way curses ride the air, along the shore after one of the floods, long strands of debris moving in the eerie lapping of the risen riverbank. Sometimes, I see men and young mothers, still brave or hungry enough to wade in up to their chests and scoop up tattered or swollen pieces of things, precious refuse.

I have taught myself to hold onto nothing—nothing but this two-wheeled contraption of mine that knows my body better than any woman or man.

Still crouching, I kept studying the toes of Ella's shoes, resting there in the dirt in front of me. Then I looked up at her face. Her mouth was slightly open, as though any answer or question she could think to give had already been snatched from her throat. Her eyes were dry, as she stood above me solid against the sun and the sky.

"I'll take you out. You don't need to know how to ride," I said in almost a whisper, still holding the bike's frame. Its own metal was starting to break down—it had that familiar feel, and a sour scent almost like blood. Most of the metal any of us has ever known is rusted and deteriorating. This destruction is everywhere you look, and denser the closer you get to the sea. Eventually, the bicycle will leave me.

Ella's voice was like a bowl, round and hollow, its sides smooth. "I can't."

"Tonight, we could go." I found myself persisting, and in that moment I was hardly able to look at her. Could she guess at the dreams I was having? I waited, trying to keep myself still inside.

She shook her head, doubtful.

"Ella, come out tonight. There's no rain—"

It was her silence, with its glitter of darkness, that caught me first. In its sharpness, I thought I could sense a sudden heat.

What could I take from Ella? I promised myself nothing. What could she take from me? I told myself I had nothing left to give, except the bicycle.

"Just this once," I said.

"I know they've asked you to keep an eye on me," she said. "But why not get out of here? Find somewhere else to go?" She was telling, not asking me, as she walked away.

"I'll come by after dark," I called out.

What I wanted then, most of all, was to swim, to wash away my fears and the heat inside me. But since the last flood, I've only let myself go in as far as my thighs, before kneeling down to wash in the shallows, wary of its deeper rivulets and watery song.

That night, I went to wait for Ella behind her hut, with my shoulder to the river, my face pulled toward its rushing sound as if by a long-time lover searching for a kiss. I called out my name to the river, and all the names of the warriors of peace, now gone. The river was running luminous under the moon and stars, shining like new metal or plastic before time began to burrow them, old and ruinous, underground.

I thought of Ella the night of the flood, alone in the hut with her baby asleep. She had told me only a few details about what happened, her memories sharp as the last shards of glass we have left in the village. The rain had been coming down for hours, but no one knew how fast the waters would rise, or how far. She had been urged by others to move onto higher ground, to get away from the river, at least for the night, but she wouldn't let herself leave. The cows were her responsibility and could not be left behind. Caring for them was the only task her brother had asked her to manage in exchange for his hut in the village. So Ella had stood in the doorway with the baby in her arms, and the animals stamping and shuddering nearby, watching the disappearing riverbank, blinking in the dampness of the air. The weight of rising water turning the ground flesh-like, a mesh of mud and grasses under the flurry of rain.

I imagined what it was like for her when the flash flood began. The river heaving up suddenly, poured heavy and sure like a gush of blood around the hut. Ella said she heard the sound of splitting and breakage strike the air, saw the low roof starting to come down. Then the water streamed inside, filling up her shelter.

The cows had panicked. Most of them went under right away, their legs splashing and kicking up mud as they sank in. Ella had moved as fast as she could, straining toward higher ground, but as the waters rose and the current strengthened, she had lost her footing and went under water, and the baby was pulled from her arms.

Remembering all this, I turned my back on that watery beast of a river. Its motion was a distraction, and its sound one that I've come to hear more and more like a kind of salivation and swallow.

I began to sing a familiar song, just loud enough so Ella would know I was there. She came outside, and I couldn't look away, couldn't see beyond her. She'd rolled her pants up her bare legs past her knees, and when she came near I could smell the smoke from the cooking fire in her hair, on her skin. I rubbed the tears from my eyes quickly so she wouldn't become a blur, lost to me.

I straddled the metal frame of the bike with one foot on either side, standing on tiptoe, waiting for her to get onto the seat just behind me, studying the shadows on the ground. She hesitated for a minute and then climbed on. I could feel the edge of her resistance but also her desire. I waited for her to choose.

She leaned in close for a minute, her face near to mine, her mouth hard, almost against my cheek, her lips there, as if to speak.

I stared at my knuckles gripping the handlebars, watching the precision of bones. Something strong. We stood together over the bicycle, hearing each other breathe. This was all there was. I reached behind slowly for her hands.

"When we get going, what we'll need is balance. If you can, keep your knees a little bent and lifted so they don't touch the ground. Hold onto me here."

I rested her fingers just above my hips and they felt light there, like the glance of a touch.

"If you'll stay sitting on the seat, I can stand on the pedals. You make the balance. I'll make us move."

I pushed us off, and we were going, faster with the weight of two bodies instead of one, down along the path toward the riverbank.

The bicycle is our last machine. The only energy it needs is our own. Ella put her arms around my waist as we sped up for a while, and pressed the side of her face to my back as I lifted and sank with the rise and fall of the pedals. It was as if she was both pulling me up and pulling me under, helping me to move faster and holding me down. I took the empty road, running first parallel and then away from the village, steering through the pale, cool moonlight and the thick hail of shadows. Miles of crumbling roads going to miles of nowhere. Where else could we go?

We listened to the birds and wolves across the night as we rode. Years ago, there used to be the sound of motors— that's what Carmen must've heard as she rode her own bike through the light and the darkness.

But now they say there is no more oil anywhere to steal or bargain for, no more gasoline, no electricity—a word that always sounded to me like the name of a beautiful woman or a constellation of stars—and no rubber even for the thinnest of spare bicycle tires. Only wind and fire to power us, water to carry it all away.

"Sonnets to Orpheus Part Two, XXIX" from *In Praise of Mortality: Selections from Rainer Maria Rilke's Duino Elegies and Sonnets to Orpheus* (Riverhead Books, 2005); reproduced with permission of translators Anita Barrows and Joanna Macy.

ACKNOWLEDGEMENTS

First and essential, thank you to Leigh Nash for publishing *Swimmers in Winter*, to Bryan Ibeas for editing the book, and to Megan Fildes, Andrew Faulkner, and Julie Wilson at Invisible Publishing.

I'm grateful to writers Emily Schultz and Thea Lim for being the first readers of the book when it was finished.

I appreciate the generosity of Anita Barrows and Joanna Macy for giving me permission to include their translation of Rainer Maria Rilke's *Sonnets to Orpheus*, Part Two, 29.

In addition, I acknowledge the support of the City of Toronto through the Toronto Arts Council, and the Ontario Arts Council.

Many thanks to Carleton Wilson for publishing my chapbook with Junction Books in which an earlier version of the story "Flood Lands" appeared, and to the co-founders of *Joyland Magazine*, Emily Schultz (again) and Brian Joseph Davis, for publishing an earlier version of the story "Swimmers in Winter" when I was starting out.

Finally, thank you to each friend along the way and to the ones who've seen me through.

INVISIBLE PUBLISHING produces fine Canadian books for those who enjoy such things. As an independent, not-for-profit publisher, our work includes building communities that sustain and encourage engaging, literary, and current writing.

Invisible Publishing has been in operation for over a decade. We released our first fiction titles in the spring of 2007, and our catalogue has come to include works of graphic fiction and non-fiction, pop culture biographies, experimental poetry, and prose.

We are committed to publishing diverse voices and experiences. In acknowledging historical and systemic barriers, and the limits of our existing catalogue, we strongly encourage LGBTQ2SIA+, Indigenous, and writers of colour to submit their work.

Invisible Publishing is also home to the Bibliophonic series of music books and the Throwback series of CanLit reissues.

If you'd like to know more, please get in touch:
info@invisiblepublishing.com

Invisible